PUPPY LOVE

by the Sea

TRACI HALL

By the Sea

AMBROSIA by the Sea
KARMA by the Sea
PUPPY LOVE by the Sea
MASQUERADE by the Sea
HOLIDAY by the Sea
FESTIVAL by the Sea
DANCING by the Sea
FOREVER by the Sea
BLUE CHRISTMAS by the Sea
RETURNING HOME by the Sea
BLOSSOMS by the Sea
BILLIONAIRE by the Sea
SANTA BABY by the Sea

AMBROSIA
By the Sea
TRACI HALL
USA TODAY BESTSELLING AUTHOR
KARMA
By the Sea
TRACI HALL
USA TODAY BESTSELLING AUTHOR
PUPPY LOVE
By the Sea
TRACI HALL
USA TODAY BESTSELLING AUTHOR
MASQUERADE
By the Sea
TRACI HALL
USA TODAY BESTSELLING AUTHOR
HOLIDAY
By the Sea
TRACI HALL
USA TODAY BESTSELLING AUTHOR
FESTIVAL
By the Sea
TRACI HALL
USA TODAY BESTSELLING AUTHOR
DANCING
By the Sea
TRACI HALL
USA TODAY BESTSELLING AUTHOR
FOREVER
By the Sea
TRACI HALL
USA TODAY BESTSELLING AUTHOR
BLUE CHRISTMAS
By the Sea
TRACI HALL
USA TODAY BESTSELLING AUTHOR
RETURNING HOME
By the Sea
TRACI HALL
USA TODAY BESTSELLING AUTHOR
BLOSSOMS
By the Sea
TRACI HALL
USA TODAY BESTSELLING AUTHOR
BILLIONAIRE
By the Sea
TRACI HALL
USA TODAY BESTSELLING AUTHOR
SANTA BABY
By the Sea
TRACI HALL
USA TODAY BESTSELLING AUTHOR
Get Them All

Chapter One

"Thanks for calling Pet Rescue," Sarah said as she answered the office phone. "How can we help you today?"

"There's a dog upstairs in my condo. *Dying*. Someone is killing the poor thing. *Killing* it." The elderly female voice on the other end wavered before stating, "I live on Ocean Drive, the Pelican Perch."

Sarah took a calming breath. She was the contracted animal control officer for a little town by the sea, population 6,000. A good portion of those residents were retired, which meant over sixty-five, with time on their hands and hearing aids they wore sporadically. She highly doubted someone was torturing their beloved pet in the lavish Pelican Perch gated community, but it was her job to check on complaints.

At 8'oclock in the morning. On a Saturday.

Sarah reached for her coffee mug, realized it was empty, and set it down with a sigh. "I'll be there within the hour, ma'am."

"You have to come *now*! That dog doesn't have an hour to live, do you hear me? What's your name? I'll report you to the manager."

I am the manager. The owner. I hear you, lady, loud and clear.

When Sarah had completed her degree in animal science, she knew she wanted to save unwanted pets. She'd known from the time she was ten and found an abandoned Collie, one who'd obviously just had puppies, on the side of the road. So when her childhood friend, Courtney Boone, ribbon-wrapped the opportunity to operate the only shelter in town, Sarah hadn't thought twice.

Maybe I should have.

"Thank you so much for calling." Sarah understood that her position in the community was all about customer service. "What was your name, ma'am?"

Click.

Sarah rolled her office chair back from the desk and

got to her feet. "It's going to be that kind of day," she told Benny. The golden Chihuahua was around twelve or so in human years, though Sarah wasn't certain. He'd been one of her first rescues, and she didn't have the heart to adopt him out. He and Pippa, a black toy Pomeranian with a gimpy back leg, lay together on a dog bed by her desk. They both got up as she made her way to the kitchen.

"I know it's a tie for what you love most," Sarah said, reaching for a plastic container. "Me or the treats." Benny knew one trick and one trick only. The Chihuahua could dance like nobody's business. "Fred Astaire, who?" He spun on his hind legs, his front paws clawing the air.

Pippa wasn't much better, but she had such a sweet face that it didn't matter. "You, pretty girl, are the product of puppy mills out of control." Pippa barked, winked her shiny black eyes and wagged her tail. It had taken a couple thousand dollars in surgery for that little miracle, and she still couldn't use her leg as anything more than a kickstand. Bad hips, the vet told her. Bad knees. Bad genes. *Beautiful dog.*

She gave them each a round pellet and scanned the kitchen counter for her keys. Nashville, her one-eyed cat, liked to play hide and seek with shiny things. Pippa spit the treat back out, nosing the green pebble across the floor toward Sarah's boot. Benny flattened his ears back against his head but he gamely choked his down. He didn't go after Pippa's reject, which told her plenty.

"I know. They don't smell good either. But they're

good for you. And cheap. It's sad but true—we're on a budget."

"Not that same old tired line," Martin (Martina without the a) sang as he came in through the back door of the facility. "You realize that we've been in business a year next month? I was hoping for a raise, doll."

Sarah laughed even as she shook her head. One month left to get the roof up to code, or they risked being shut down. "Me, too."

Benny and Pippa barked a greeting, prancing around Martin's legs while Nashville lurked from a shadowy corner, the truck keys in her mouth. The gray and white tabby meowed around them, whiskers twitching, taunting, as she stared Sarah down. "Give me those, Nash." The cat darted out of reach, tail high.

Martin was of Hispanic descent, thin, tanned and smoothly waxed for the weekend shows he did at Lipz, where he played Diana Ross better than Diana. She guessed his age around thirty-five, but he'd never said. "You're the owner. You're supposed to be broke for a few years. Me?" He flashed his show-stopping smile. "I've got the girls to keep in kibble."

"I can barely afford the twelve bucks an hour you get now." Martin had a townhouse filled with cats, dogs and birds that he'd rescued over the years. Somehow the menagerie all managed to get along—his only rule was that they had to be female.

He walked over and kissed her cheek. "I know,

sugar. I know. So where are you off to already?"

"A woman from the Pelican Perch called to tell me someone is torturing an animal upstairs in her condo. Killing it, she said. And I need to hurry, or she'll call my manager."

Martin looked at her over the slim bridge of his cosmetically altered nose. "This is why I am glad to get my meager paycheck. You get the headache. My mother told me to go into business for myself, but no, I've seen the troubles you go through."

Sarah acted like she wasn't going anywhere near the cat, then swooped in behind to get the keys from her mouth. "Gotchya!" Nashville yowled her protest, leaping to the table in the kitchen to clean her ears as if she'd let Sarah have them on purpose. "You know, I think I'm going to invest in a heavier ring. One Nashville can't lift."

Martin waved his hand at the cat. "She'll find a way, stubborn thing."

Sarah noticed Martin's belt. She'd implemented a dress code so that they presented a united, professional front. Khaki or navy shorts or slacks. Beige, white or navy button-up or polo. Simple. Sneakers were all right, but she preferred her brown leather ankle boots.

"Speaking of stubborn, Martin, what is that around your waist?"

He opened the cupboard above the coffee maker, searching for a mug. "A belt?" Martin peeked at her around the door.

"Is that glitter?"

"There is nothing in the handbook about belts. I checked. Besides, what's the matter with a splash of color? You're trying to suffocate my creativity!"

Sarah snickered. "If you've found a way to creatively clean the dog pens, then you know what? Glitter away." Clasping the keys in her hand, she searched for her purse. The dogs jumped at her feet while Nashville pointedly ignored her. "Martin, those treats are so bad, Pippa won't eat them."

"That *is* bad." He sniffed a green pellet from the jar on the counter and tossed it in the trash. "I don't blame her. I'll pick some up on my lunch break."

"No, Martin, I'll do it."

"Want me to give you a couple bucks? Splurge on the name brand?"

"Those are filled with crap."

"You aren't going to get quality for cheap, Chiquita."

The phone rang and Martin ran to answer it, ending the argument. "Thank you for calling Pet Rescue, how can we help you today?"

Sarah found her purse beneath the newspaper she hadn't had time to read. Office hours were eight to six, though she was on call for emergencies around the clock. She'd barely finished one cup of joe.

"Oh no, ma'am, that won't be necessary," Martin said in a soothing voice as he sat in the office chair. "Of course, Mrs. Drummel. Our best officer is already on her way."

With that, Sarah scooted out the front door so she didn't make Martin a liar.

She drove the five blocks down Ocean Blvd, turning right into the gated community of Pelican Perch.

What to expect? Opting to keep her tools in the truck, Sarah parked in the visitor's section and took her leather gloves from the center console. She climbed out, stuffing her gloves into her back pocket, and went inside the coral-colored high-rise. Air conditioning hummed around the white marble lobby. Floral carpet runners assigned a path toward the desk, or the bank of elevators.

A piercing cry winged through the vents and the man behind the desk met her gaze. "We've been waiting for you," he said, rising from the chair and offering his hand. "I'm Bob."

The heartbreaking cries made her chest pound in empathy. "Wow. I'm Sarah Murphy. How long has this been going on?"

"An hour. We've knocked on the door. No answer. I've called up to the unit, but I don't think anybody is home. In this instance, I can unlock the door for you to get the animal out of the apartment. I'll go with you. God knows what we're gonna find."

Sarah thought about going out to her truck for a net, but the cry was so sharp and filled with pain that she didn't want to waste any more time.

About fifty, Bob wore a white long-sleeved button up shirt with a black tie and black work pants. He headed toward the elevator bank, head down. "Winter people," he muttered.

"Excuse me?" Sarah asked, not sure if he was speaking to her or not.

"Owner normally stays off and on over the winter." Bob shrugged. "He's moved in permanent. The last few months." Reeking of disapproval, the man hit the button and they rode the elevator to the sixteenth floor.

"Penthouse?" she asked. This was so not her life.

"People think they got money they can do whatever they want. But we don't hold with animal cruelty here at the Pelican Perch."

The sharp cries increased in volume, tearing at her heart strings. "I can see why Mrs. Drummel called. This is terrible…"She took her gloves from her pocket.

"It started off real faint, occasional, but got louder in the past half hour." They left the elevator and the cries echoed around the foyer. There was only one apartment on this floor. The best of the best.

Sarah shook her head, angry on behalf of whatever was hurting behind those doors. She walked over and knocked, three times, hard. "Animal control," she said in a stern voice. "Open the door."

The cries became louder, as if crossing a hall, coming toward her. The lock slid back, and Sarah braced herself for what came her way. She should have grabbed a bite stick from the truck simply for defense. What kind of person could stand to hurt an animal like that?

The door opened inward and Sarah's sharp words caught in her throat.

A little girl, maybe seven or eight, all big teeth and curly dark brown hair, stared at her in obvious distress. Wide, brown eyes glistened as she cried along with the tiny Yorkshire Terrier puppy in her hands. The puppy looked to be about six weeks old. She held it awkwardly, stiffly, toward Sarah.

"Paisley won't stop crying," the girl said, tears streaming down olive-toned cheeks. She hiccupped and waited for someone to help her.

Bob coughed into his fist and looked away, all gruff and tough man gone in the face of the little girl's plight. Sarah realized it would be up to her to fix it.

Putting her gloves away, she dropped to her knees and held out her hands for the shrieking puppy. "Let me see what's going on here." Sarah felt its nose. *Hot.* A fever? Peering down to its mouth, she got a whiff of something rotten.

Grateful for her time as a vet assistant, Sarah probed the small jaw and found a bleeding puppy tooth covered by infected gums. Curable, but obviously painful. "All right honey," she said to the little girl. "It's all right. Paisley has a toothache."

The girl sniffed and swiped a hand under her eyes. "She does?" She looked to where Sarah pointed and sighed, her small body leaning against Sarah. "I thought Paisley hated me. She doesn't cry when Daddy holds her."

Sarah hid a smile. Sweet that she thought her dad was a hero. *Where was he?* "What's your name?" Sarah cupped Paisley in her hands for security, snuggling the exhausted puppy close to her chest until the poor thing quieted down.

"Bella." She took a breath, her narrow shoulders visible in her yellow sundress. "IsabellaMariaBlancheRodriguesdeSilva."

Sarah couldn't help but be charmed as she untangled Isabella and Maria Rodrigues out of the compounded name, recited in perfect English. *No wonder she went by Bella.* "Is your mom home? Or your dad?"

Tears started again. "Mama is dead. Daddy promised he'd come right home! I called him," she said through fresh sobs. "I called him *forever* ago."

Bella didn't have a mom? Why would her dad leave his kid home by herself to take care of a sick puppy? Wasn't she too young to be by herself, anyway? Sarah reminded herself that she was in a world where just about anything could be bought. "Do you have a nanny?"

Bella softly touched the silky fur, relaxing against Sarah while not answering the question. "My puppy doesn't like me. Will Paisley die too?"

Sarah didn't even want to connect what those two things might mean. Surely this beautiful kid didn't believe her mother hadn't liked her? "If we take the puppy to the vet, she should be okay. Bella, where is your nanny?"

"She went home and left me here." Bella sniffled loudly. "Daddy was really mad and said she was going to be *fired.*" She put her finger to her lips, swearing Sarah and Bob to secrecy. "He said some bad words."

Bob chuckled. "I bet."

"He's supposed to be home." Bella's voice quivered with emotion. "Where is he?"

Sarah decided that keeping Bella and the puppy calmed down was the first step toward figuring out what to do next. They couldn't stay in the foyer all day. "How about we sit on the couch and I can show you how to hold Paisley so that she'll sleep until your dad gets here?"

Bella's eyes rounded and she clutched Sarah's arm. "Don't leave me. Don't go."

Babysitting was not on her list of duties, but no way could Sarah turn her back on this little girl. "I'll just get you settled in, okay?" What was her dad doing that he couldn't get home? Golfing? "Where is your dad, hon?"

"Work." Bella sucked in her lower lip. "Just for a little while."

So not out playing a few rounds... Sarah acknowledged that circumstances seemed to have created a tough situation, but a job was not more important than your kid. Period. Her protective instincts kicked in. "All right. I'll stay until he comes home."

"I'll go back down, then," the manager said.

"Isabella, my name is Bob. If you need me, just use the house phone to call 315. That rings at the front desk. I can help you."

Bella's lower lip trembled as she nodded. "I'm not supposed to talk to strangers."

"Well, now, we aren't strangers anymore, right?" Bob held out his hand, and he and Bella shook on it. "I've got a granddaughter about your age."

She smiled, the tears forgotten. "Can she come and play?"

"Madison lives in New York."

"Oh." Bella's face fell.

"But she visits for the summer. Maybe you girls can go to the beach together."

"I can ask my daddy," Bella said from Sarah's side.

Bob pushed the button to return to the lobby just as the elevator doors opened.

Sarah, still kneeling with the puppy at her chest and Bella at her shoulder, caught her breath as one of the most handsome men she'd ever seen walked out of the car. Her stomach knotted as she recognized the thick black hair cut to the neck in a relaxed style that screamed high-end salon. Dark brows and a prominent nose set above a mouth meant for kissing—when it wasn't thin with worry, like now.

Franco de Silva. Stunned, she looked at the puppy, then *Isabella*, and rose to her full height. Five foot six wasn't much compared to his over six feet, but she wouldn't let that stop her from giving him an earful. *Figured it was him.* Her nemesis.

Bella left her side and shouted "Daddy!" in such a gleeful voice that Sarah bit her tongue. A few months ago Franco de Silva had come into town, throwing money around and re-opening the pet store it had taken her six months to close. The previous owners had run a puppy mill out of the premium downtown space, forging pedigrees and selling over-bred dogs to unsuspecting tourists.

As if sensing Sarah's emotional turmoil, the puppy woke up and continued its gut-wrenching cries. She brought Paisley to her chest and made soothing noises.

Franco's head dipped as he took in her uniform and the puppy in her hands, barely glancing at Sarah's face. He put his hand on his daughter's small shoulder, rubbing her back. "Are you all right, Bella? I'm sorry you were frightened."

"Yes, yes. Sarah said Paisley has a tooth ache."

His furious gaze snagged hers and held it. "Sarah Murphy," he said between gritted teeth, his throat red with suppressed anger. "What are you doing here?"

She refused to back down from the contempt radiating from him, though it stung. "We got a disturbance call. Animal Control."

"I know what you do." Calm. Cool. Controlled.

She knew her weekly visits angered him, but she wouldn't let his money, charm or good looks stop her from doing the right thing. "My job." Sarah thought it was too much of a coincidence that he'd swooped in and opened another puppy store. Designer dogs were easy money. Enough to afford this penthouse? "I protect animals that can't protect themselves."

There was probably a reason Paisley had bad teeth. Disreputable breeders tossed a mix together based on looks rather than what was healthy, all for the big bucks.

They stared at one another, tension screeching like nails down a chalk board.

"You are on the wrong trail," Franco said, his eyes narrowed. "I've got the citation you gave us taped by the register. My staff knows to call the *real police* if you ever set foot in my store again."

Chapter Two

Sarah rocked from one foot to the next, humming to keep the puppy calm. She remembered giving Franco the citation his first week in business. He'd left a bucket of cleaner out along with a mop. While she'd looked for other potential signs that the puppy mill was back in operation, it was all she could get him for—a possible health hazard if the puppies were to drink the toxic cleaning solution. She'd been sick to her stomach, wondering if he was new management for an old scheme. "It was just a warning ticket."

He opened his mouth as if to argue, then looked at Bob and Bella and closed it. The puppy quieted as Sarah massaged its belly. *Probably hungry.*

"Paisley has an infected baby tooth, which has more than likely stopped her from eating. She's hurting and hungry, a bad combination. I can recommend a vet, if you need one." She tried not to take Franco's anger personally.

"I have the best," Franco said, moving toward his front door with Bella attached at his denim-clad leg.

Sarah clenched her jaw. *The best?* She regretted any acrimony between them, but she wouldn't let another illegal mill pop up. Her weekly checks at his store had shown nothing out of line. "Money can't buy everything."

Franco scowled at her, holding out his hands. "Give me my dog."

Paisley fit inside Franco's large palm, instantly quiet as she nudged her nose between his thumb and forefinger. His touch soothed the puppy, just as he'd soothed his daughter. Sarah observed how different he was here compared to the pet store. *Can I blame him for being a jerk after I threatened to shut him down?*

Bella clung to her dad's leg, her bare feet curled against the thin carpet. "It was very nice to meet you, Bella."

"Bye, Sarah," the little girl said. "Come back and visit me!"

Not likely, she thought with a pang. Confused

emotions tangled around her, mainly empathy for Bella. And there was a glimmer of understanding regarding Franco, who was now more than just an arrogant, handsome pet store owner.

Franco said nothing, though his brown eyes, eyes just like Bella's, spoke volumes. He was angry she had intruded on his home turf. They both knew she had every right to check out his shop.

Bella went inside their condo without a backward glance. "Daddy, I'll get the carrier so we can see Dr. Wilton."

"You use Dr. Wilton?" Sarah asked with surprise. It was her vet of choice, too.

"I told you, I use the best." Franco looked behind him to make sure that Bella was not in hearing distance then he spoke through clenched teeth in a voice pitched just low enough for Sarah. "Don't come back here again. I'll have you arrested for trespassing." He closed the door in her face.

Sarah stepped back in a huff, cheeks stinging. "Take care of your puppy, and I won't have to," she muttered, suddenly conscious of Bob holding the elevator for her. He'd witnessed the entire exchange.

"No telling what's what with the rich and famous," Bob said as they got back into the elevator. He was obviously curious but too polite to ask.

"Franco de Silva doesn't care for me," Sarah said with an indifferent shrug that hid her tumultuous feelings.

"You know he owns that designer dog store? de Silva's Diamond Dogs. What do you mean, famous?" He was hot enough to be an actor, but she'd never seen him in anything. She would have remembered.

"Not him. His wife. Bianca Rodrigues was a daytime drama actress in Brazil. My girlfriend showed me some pictures on the Internet. Very beautiful. I guess she died of a drug overdose. Not sure if it was intentional or not." He jerked his thumb upward toward the penthouse. "Just over a year ago."

"Poor Bella." Sarah pulled her gloves from her back pocket, twisting the soft leather. Jennifer Murphy nagged about eating right and burned the Thanksgiving turkey, but Sarah couldn't imagine her mother not being a phone call away. Nope, money was not everything.

And what about Franco? At the shop, he epitomized arrogance. A need to be in control. He wore machismo like cologne and Sarah avoided guys like that as if she had an allergy.

They didn't usually go for her, either. She was proud of her independence and felt no need to apologize for being female.

"Cute kid," Bob said. "I didn't realize she lived in the building, but I don't normally work weekends."

The elevator dinged at the third floor and they picked up an older gentleman with a brown panama hat and plaid shorts. He nodded to Sarah, said hello to Bob, and stepped back against the wall.

The doors closed, and Sarah saw herself in the silver reflection. Blonde hair, khaki shorts. Work boots. Plain and boring. While Franco was so good-looking that she told herself, in those odd moments when, for no reason at all, she imagined him smiling at her instead of sneering, he couldn't be real. Yet seeing him with his daughter, so tender and caring? The gentle way he'd cupped the puppy in his gigantic hands? Did something to her heart that messed with what her head knew to be true.

He'd moved right into that old pet store and slapped a fresh coat of paint on the walls, as if that would cover up the crimes that had been committed there. He'd known what happened—she'd told him in minute detail.

He'd shouted something about Brazilian integrity.

What a mess.

They reached the bottom floor and Sarah nodded to both men as she got off first. "Call me if you need anything, Bob."

"Thanks for coming," the manager said.

Once in the truck, she dialed the office.

"Thanks for calling Pet Rescue, how may we help you today?"

"Martin, you are never going to believe what just happened."

A few hours later, Franco sat on the couch next to Bella,

watching cartoons in Spanish. He usually made her watch them in English, but she was so upset about Paisley having to stay overnight at the vet's that he didn't push the issue.

"Will Dr. Wilton pull Paisley's tooth?"

"Yes," Franco said, tugging on one of Bella's curls. "It is a baby tooth, like yours."

"Will the tooth fairy come?"

Franco scratched his jaw. Would the tooth fairy make an appearance for a puppy? He'd have to check with the vet. Dr. Wilton, a gorgeous woman of about sixty, had steered him around some sticky issues already. Where to send Bella to school, where to buy her uniforms. A good pediatrician. It had been a blessed day when he'd found her business card in the chamber of commerce.

"We can ask Dr. Wilton."

Bella nodded, the answer satisfying her for the moment. He, who'd made millions, relied on the kindness of strangers when it came to advice for his daughter.

This single parenting was new for him, though as it happened, his wife had mostly left Bella with nannies. He remembered his surprise when Bianca had announced her pregnancy over caviar and champagne. *Supposedly an accident.* She'd acted horrified, but then again, Bianca was a professional actress. How could he have forgotten that?

He'd expected they'd be a family. Dinners, church, vacations. Oh, how his wife had lied. Covered up. Deceit and betrayal burned his heart and he rubbed at the poisonous ache in his chest.

Franco thanked God every day that Bianca hadn't taken their daughter with her while she bought drugs, or did them. Absent parenting was better than putting his baby at risk.

He'd assumed his wife wanted to spend her free time with their only child, as he did, but it seemed Bianca had demons driving her that he knew nothing about. He liked to party as much as the next man. Brandy, good cigars. He enjoyed food and amusing company, but he always looked forward to being home with Bella.

Franco's business called for him to travel. He was a chef to the stars. He hadn't been there when his six-year-old daughter found her mother "sleeping" in the bathtub.

He'd promised himself then that he would never leave his daughter again. Not looking back, he sold their holdings in Brazil and brought Bella here, where she remembered hunting for shells at the ocean's surf and looking at sea turtles. Not a single memory of her dead mother.

"I like Dr. Wilton. She's nice." Bella snuggled next to him, her eyes on the dancing teddy bears.

She'd been sent by angels, he was sure of it. His daughter always wanted a dog but they'd never had pets because of Bianca's allergies so he'd promised her a puppy when they came to Florida. Somehow he'd ended up with an entire store. de Silva's Diamond Dogs.

"Yes, she is." He'd gone to Dr. Wilton once he'd bought the old pet store business, proposing that she give him a discount on vet services if he used her for healthy puppy certification. She'd warned him that the previous owners had been running a sham operation. He had the time and patience to turn the place around, he'd told her. It helped that he didn't need the money.

What he needed was a community. A place where he and Bella could heal.

After Bianca's death, news reporters had stalked his daughter for pictures of her grief. They'd broken into her private school. Hidden in trees to capture her face for the tabloids. Bianca had been a loved celebrity.

And a royal bitch.

There were so many questions he'd never have answers to. Franco hugged Bella to him, blinking tears from his eyes. "Want Daddy to make you lunch, princess?"

"Yes, please. Grilled cheese with tomato soup."

He buried his face in his daughter's hair. He, chef to the stars of Europe, who made dishes rich in creams and savory sauces, was reduced to grilled cheese. "Cracked wheat bread all right with you?"

She nodded, engrossed in the program. "Can we invite Sarah to come back for lunch?"

God, no, he thought, immediately picturing Sarah Murphy. Fair blonde hair and freckles, green eyes the color of the tropical Amazon, and knobby knees beneath her serviceable khaki shorts.

The animal control officer stopped by once a week,

letting him know she was watching. It got under his skin, even though he understood her reasons. He would never stoop to something illegal or immoral. But would she even give him a chance? No. She slapped him with a bogus citation just because she could.

Sarah set his nerves on edge and he found himself doing a double-take out the shop's windows whenever a woman with her shade of blonde hair walked by. She challenged him, refusing to be charmed. Not that he'd tried too hard. No, she brought out his worst.

"She's nice." Bella slid a sideways glance at him.

He'd taken a hit to the gut, getting off the elevator to see his precious Bella leaning so trustingly against his enemy. Bella wouldn't understand why Sarah was determined to close his shop. He'd asked Dr. Wilton about her, and the vet had nothing but glowing words. Ran a no-kill shelter, volunteered in the community. Hired by the city to answer animal complaints, which was why she'd shown up at his home this morning. She'd looked so soft, so caring, until she'd recognized him and then her entire demeanor had changed. Why did it bother him, whether or not the woman liked him?

Bella patted his cheek. "Isn't she, Daddy? Isn't Sarah nice?"

"Yes, yes, Bella. She is nice." He gritted his teeth and got up from the couch. *A nice pain in the butt.*

Instead of staying put, Bella followed him, climbing up the barstool to the high counter overlooking the square kitchen. "Can I butter the bread, Daddy?"

"Sure, princess." He got the tub of whipped butter from the refrigerator, six slices of bread and a plate, along with a butter knife. "Remember to get the corners."

She grinned. "I know, or the bread won't toast."

"Pretty soon, you will be making the grilled cheese all by yourself," he told her. How he cherished this time with Isabella, sensing that childhood would be gone before he was ready. He had memories of cooking with his mother, of being encouraged to create. It led him to a lucrative career, following his passion.

"As good as you, Daddy?"

He lifted a spatula from the drawer. "Better."

She giggled, carefully spreading butter to each corner of the bread, the tip of her tongue poking out as she concentrated. "No way."

"Way." He took out sharp cheddar, provolone and pepper jack. His daughter liked to eat, which made cooking even the simple things fun.

"I think Sarah is pretty. I wish I had blonde hair."

The last thing Franco needed was his daughter to form an attachment to the woman who thought he'd knowingly sell unhealthy puppies for his own profit. "Bella, you have beautiful dark hair. It matches your eyelashes and your eyebrows. You would look funny with blonde hair."

"Or purple hair?" she asked with a snicker.

"Especially purple hair."

"But it looked pretty on Kelly Osbourne."

"How do you remember that, princess? You met her over a year ago." He'd cooked for many famous families, and they'd come to pay their respects at Bianca's funeral.

"It was pretty. She was nice, too." Bella shrugged and went on to the next piece of bread. "Can I pierce my nose?"

Franco, who had been getting a frying pan from the bottom cupboard, stood up so fast he hit his head against the counter. "Ouch, er." *Damn it.* "No, you are not going to get your nose pierced!"

Bella laughed from her tummy. "Just kidding."

He exhaled and leaned against the sink. "You think you're funny? A comedienne?"

"Want to hear my knock knock joke?"

"Where did you learn a knock knock joke?" He turned the stove on and added butter to the pan. "Cartoons?"

"My teacher at school. She has gray hair, Daddy, and she's not always very nice."

"But she teaches you jokes?"

"It goes like this..."

Franco bowed his head, his heart bursting with love for his daughter. How could his wife have chosen drugs and suicide over this?

Chapter Three

Sarah sat at her desk, wishing the numbers in her checking account had a few extra zeros in it. No matter how hard she stared at the computer screen, they never changed. The phone rang and she answered, glad for the reprieve. "Thanks for calling Pet Rescue, how can we help you today?"

"Hi Sarah, this is Bob, the manager at the Pelican Perch."

"Hello, Bob. Is the puppy still a problem?" She glanced at the wall calendar that had been her Grand

Opening giveaway. "It's been a week."

"It's not about that. Haven't heard a peep. Mr. de Silva and Bella are really good at taking care of her. I've seen the puppy since then. Very friendly, now that she's not in any more pain. Which is why I've called. Sort of. Mrs. Drummel was thinking about getting a cat, and she wondered if you had any for adoption."

Nashville yowled from behind the file cabinet. Sarah shook her head, knowing she was stuck with this particular cantankerous feline. "Does she want a kitten, or a full grown cat?" She knew each of her animal residents well, down to their eating habits and nap times. "Someone abandoned a litter by the pier last week and I've got them all inoculated and healthy. Then I've got a neutered black cat, about ten, white paws. A real hugger."

Bob cleared his throat. "She wants a white one."

Sarah tried not to laugh. She imagined Mrs. Drummel might be particular, herself. "We've got a five-year old female that's mostly white. She's got gray at the tip of her tail and her hind paws."

"I'll ask her."

"There's a picture of Miss Priss on the website. Of all the animals, if you want to help Mrs. Drummel browse."

"Great idea, Sarah. Thanks!"

She hung up the phone and went back into the rooms where the animals were kept. The old warehouse connected to the front office gave her plenty of room for her rescued pets. Lots of light, with an indoor area to run around. Matching people with pets was something she really enjoyed and right now she had the cats, three mutts, a rabbit and an iguana all looking for homes.

Food cost money, the roof had to be fixed, and she had no idea how to get the cash she needed—but she would go down fighting. The animals relied on her and it satisfied something in her DNA to help.

Martin came in the back door with the three dogs on leashes, all of them panting. His thin belt reflected the light coming in from the windows. "Woo! It's getting hot out there. Were you looking for me?"

"No, I just was checking on Miss Priss back here. We might have a taker." Sarah walked to the cage where the white cat slept at the very top of the cat climber. Six feet tall with carpet branches, the pole allowed the cats to climb and scratch. Sarah opened the screened-frame door and walked in. "Hey there, sweetie."

The white cat had beautiful blue eyes and a slender build that had been on the point of emaciation when Sarah had rescued her from a Dumpster. She meowed in greeting, curling her fluffy tail around her hind leg.

"She's had all of her shots," Martin said, letting the dogs get a drink of water from the big bowl on the floor. "And she's spayed. I'll miss her pretty face."

Sarah turned to Martin with a shake of her head. "You, my friend, have enough animals at home."

"She would have fit in nicely." Martin turned on his

heel and opened the doors for the dogs to go back into their crates. They did, the morning exercise demanding an immediate nap. "A Diva born on the wrong side of the tracks. Who is the lucky buyer?"

"I'm not sure if it's a sale yet, but it's that older lady at the Pelican Perch who wanted to call my manager last week."

Martin looked heavenward. "Sweet thing decided she needed a pet after all of that excitement?"

"Maybe so," Sarah laughed.

He leaned toward her and winked. "Any word from Franco de Silva?"

Sarah blushed. "No. Why would there be?"

"Wishful thinking on my part. I saw him, you know. After hearing your story last week, I had to check out the puppy store, and honey," Martin waved his hand over his face, "he is scrumptious."

Sarah agreed, but to herself. He'd been making appearances every night in her dreams, spearing her with fury in his brown eyes. She'd witnessed his gentleness. It was so at odds with the man she thought she knew that her mind was having a tough time sorting out which Franco de Silva was the real Franco de Silva. "What did you think of the shop?"

"Clean, bright, classy. Not a hint of Lysol anywhere. Hand sanitizer stations, attendants to watch how customers held the dogs."

"Good." She nodded, truly wanting the best for the

animals in Franco's care. "I really don't want to be a hard-ass, but I can't look away if the puppies are being mistreated."

"New owner. I think things will be all right." He started to turn away, but then came back with a mischievous smile. "However, I'd be glad to take over the weekly check."

Sarah laughed and pushed her friend on the arm. "Franco threatened to call the cops, so you might have to." She sighed and gave Miss Priss one more ear scratch before heading into the office as the phone rang again. "I'm not sure it's worth the drama, especially if he's on the up and up." Racing to reach it before they hung up, she was somewhat breathless as she answered. "Pet Rescue."

"Sarah? It's Bob. Mrs. Drummel has decided on the white one with the gray tips."

She sank into her office chair with relief. "Wonderful. We have a set adoption fee, though we are mostly run by donation," she began.

"We saw that on the site. We've filled out the application online already, too. Mrs. Drummel requests that you deliver the cat, if you can? She will pay extra. She would need cat food, litter and a collar as well."

Sarah mentally added up the charges and smiled. "My pleasure. I can drop the cat off around three, if that is all right?"

"Sure. And thank you!"

Sarah hit the intercom on the desk that went from the

front office to the warehouse. "Martin, could you get the complete package prepared for Miss Priss? She's moving up!"

Heading into the kitchen, Benny and Pippa hot on her heels, Sarah looked at the bag of treats Martin had thoughtfully brought in. She read the back and cringed at the ingredients. "How hard can it be to make these things healthy and tasty?"

Pippa and Benny barked for a chance to taste the treat. Sarah gave them each one from the bag and they wagged their tails. "You know there isn't anything good in there for you?" They didn't seem to care.

Wondering if she could just make them herself, she used the iPad on the counter to search homemade doggy treats, jotting down a few ingredients on a sticky pad. "I have to be able to do this better."

Using the money she'd get from Mrs. Drummel, Sarah decided to try a few different batches. "Healthy can still taste good," she told her dogs.

They didn't look convinced.

Nashville leaped to the desk and groomed her hind leg. Was it possible to make them for cats, too? She might try it, depending on how the dog treats turned out.

Martin came out of the warehouse to the front office with Miss Priss glaring daggers from behind the bars of a pink cat carrier. "I've told her we love her," he said, his voice thick with emotion.

"Of course we do!" Sarah took the carrier. "Martin,

we can't keep them all. Other people need to know the unconditional love of a pet."

"When you put it like that…I already stacked the supplies in your truck." He dabbed at his lower eyelid.

"Thank you. Do you want to come?"

"No, no. We've said our good-byes." His sharp eye noticed the hot pink sticky note on her purse. "What's that?"

"When I get back, I'm baking."

"Here?"

"I don't have any cookie sheets or anything at my apartment." She didn't really spend much time in the kitchen.

"I didn't know you could use anything other than the microwave."

"It's a good thing you're cute," she said, heading out the door.

The South Florida heat walloped her in the face but she pushed forward. She opened the truck, slid in, and put the carrier next to her on the floor, immediately cranking the air conditioner.

Miss Priss chose to voice her opinion of the move with a loud and scratchy yowl. No amount of sweet talk from Sarah helped.

By the time she made it through the gate, parked and lifted Miss Priss' carrier, Sarah was certain Mrs. Drummel would send the cat right back.

"Please be sweet, Miss Priss. This could be your

forever home. It's a lot nicer than the Dumpster."

Bob met her at the door, opening it wide. "Sarah! We were waiting for you."

She followed Bob's gesture and saw a short woman with tight white curls and lots of jewelry get up from the chair in the foyer, her glossy white purse over her arm. Sarah lifted the carrier and the cat stopped yowling as she took in her surroundings. Marble, air conditioning. The smell of money.

"Mrs. Drummel," Sarah said with a broad smile. "So nice to finally meet you!"

The woman ignored her for the cat carrier, making steady progress across the tile floor. She shuffled her steps, but walked without a cane. "Is this the one? Let me see."

Sarah set the carrier on a giant round table next to an ornate silk floral arrangement. Mrs. Drummel, wearing a white t-shirt, pink shorts and pink sneakers, patted the pink carrier with what might have been approval. "Do I get to keep this?"

"Sure, if you want it. I'll just have to add the replacement cost to your bill."

She waved her ringed hand. "I've got my checkbook."

Bob went to the woman's other side as she opened the carrier. Miss Priss blinked slowly, taking in her new owner.

Mrs. Drummel reached in and gently pulled the

white cat out, cradling Miss Priss in her arms. "Hello, beautiful."

Miss Priss, thank all the stars, purred, and Sarah breathed a sigh of relief.

Just then the door swung open and a yippy barking sound collided with a little girl's laughter.

"Bob, look what I did at school today!"

Bella, dressed in her school uniform of navy blue shorts and a red polo shirt, ran for Bob, the dog in her arms barking with excitement. The cat squirmed from Mrs. Drummel's grasp, leaping free with a terrified yowl.

No, no, no! Sarah captured the clawing cat mid-air before Miss Priss landed on the marble tile and broke a leg or something.

Somehow she was able to get the cat to her chest, but not before Miss Priss scratched down her chin. *Ouch.*

Bella stopped talking as she realized what happened. Her brown eyes widened with fear. "Sarah, you're bleeding!"

"What's going on here?" Franco asked. His accent was barely discernible as he joined his daughter, who snuggled Paisley protectively to her body.

"Your dog frightened my cat," Mrs. Drummel announced, her back straight, her finger shaky as she pointed at Franco.

Sarah crammed an indignant Miss Priss back in the carrier, digging a napkin from her pocket to press against her stinging chin.

"I'm sure she didn't do it on purpose." Franco's entire demeanor was smooth as he answered, from voice to body language. Probably got himself out of many a situation just using that charm, Sarah thought. "She's a puppy."

Mrs. Drummel sniffed, not quite immune to Franco's deep, honeyed tones. "Puppies are like children. They need training."

Franco's shoulders tightened at the rebuke. He wore tailored jeans and a tucked-in black polo. A black leather belt and black leather loafers completed his "casual" attire. His dark, wavy hair was kept from his face by sunglasses on his head.

"It was an accident, that's all." Sarah dabbed once more at her chin, shoved the napkin back into her pocket and gestured for Bob to assist.

The manager came forward and tapped the pink carrier. "Let's get Miss Priss settled, shall we, Mrs. Drummel? I can walk you back to your condo."

"Yes," the old woman said, her attention diverted. "I've got her new home all ready." Mrs. Drummel reached into her shiny white purse and pulled out a leather checkbook, tearing out a pre-written check. "I've made it for three hundred."

Sarah blinked, hoping she hadn't misunderstood. "That's more than the bill."

"Put the rest toward the shelter. Don't jostle that carrier, Bob. And you, little girl, be careful with that puppy."

"Yes, ma'am," Bella said, slipping her hand into her dad's.

Franco's jaw clenched but he nodded his head at the older lady, who put her arm through Bob's.

"Thank you very much, Mrs. Drummel. I'll leave the food and supplies by the desk." Sarah wished she'd had kinder thoughts toward the older lady. The extra money would come in handy for sure.

Bob nodded. "Sure. Thanks again, Sarah, for delivering Miss Priss."

"I don't like that name," Mrs. Drummel said. "I was thinking Jasmine. Isn't that lovely?"

"Perfect," Bob agreed.

Sarah, frazzled again, forced herself to smile at Franco. It was easier to reach down and pet Paisley. "Hi, Bella. Good day at school?"

"*Gosto, sim.* I mean, yes. Sarah, you need a bandage for your chin. We have one upstairs in our bathroom. In the medicine cabinet. Don't we, Daddy?"

Sarah pulled the shredded napkin from her pocket and dabbed at the cut. He looked perfect and she was a disaster. Not that she cared. *Right?*

Franco gritted his teeth. "We do, but I'm sure Sarah will be fine as soon as she gets back to her office. Or home. Whatever."

Bella frowned. "But her napkin is all red! And we have the sticky stuff that stops *bacteria.*"

Sarah felt Franco's animosity toward her. She'd caused it, by giving him the citation. Uncertain how to change things, Sarah said, "Thank you, Bella. It's very thoughtful, but I'll be fine. I have a first-aid kit in my truck. "

"See, Bella?" Franco took his hand from his daughter's and put it on Bella's shoulder, guiding her toward the elevators. "Sarah is fine." Then he removed his sunglasses from their perch on his head and stared at her chin.

She didn't like his scrutiny and she wasn't at all prepared for him to reach over and pull a piece of napkin free.

"Ouch!" Sarah shivered—partly because that freaking hurt, and a little bit due to his close proximity. He made her nervous, plain and simple.

"It looks pretty deep," he said, as if she'd done it on purpose. "Maybe you'd better come up and clean it out."

"I'll be fine," she squeaked before backing into the table.

"Please, Sarah?" Bella asked. "We can watch cartoons and my daddy could make us grilled cheese sandwiches."

Pushing away from the table, Sarah pressed the napkin to her chin, wishing she had something to hide her blushing face. "I'll be okay, really. And I have to get back to work."

Bella set Paisley on the ground, keeping her hand on

the puppy's pink leash. "What do you do, Sarah? My mama was an actress. She had allergies."

Sarah glanced at Franco before answering Bella. "Nothing as glamorous." She pointed to her shorts and ankle boots. "I help animals. I'm here because Mrs. Drummel just adopted a cat from my shelter."

"Can we get a cat, Daddy?"

"You have a puppy, Bella." Franco's eyes traveled from the top of her head to her feet, then came up again to read the Pet Rescue logo at her left shoulder. "That's enough for now."

"Don't forget your pet store full of designer puppies," Sarah said, wondering why she needled Franco. Maybe she wanted him to feel as unsettled as she did.

"Designer? What does that mean?" Bella asked, looking up at her dad.

She immediately saw that any empathy Franco might have been feeling toward her over her injury was gone. He blinked, all hard edges once more. "Time to go, Bella. You and I can finish this conversation another time, Sarah. I'll be calling."

Great. An ass-reaming she probably deserved.

"Looking forward to it," she said, wishing she hadn't lost control. "Bye, Bella. Franco."

He used his tone to draw a line in the sand. "That is Mr. de Silva to you."

Sarah's chin stung but not as much as her pride. She pushed open the door that led outside and stomped to her truck. *I know better than that.*

"Daddy, are you mad at Sarah?"

Franco seethed inside the elevator. "No, honey." Mad was way too tame a word for how he felt about Sarah Murphy.

"You sounded mad," his daughter insisted.

"I was worried about her chin." There'd been an instant, a second, that Franco wanted to help Sarah. Offer her comfort. Touch her arm, her hair—then she had to go and say what she did about his "designer" puppies.

What was that about? He'd been prepared all week for battle if she stepped into his store, right down to the dialogue they'd exchange. And somehow, in his traitorous mind, their heated argument always ended with a passionate kiss. She hadn't come in. She'd sent her assistant, Martin, instead.

He clenched his fists at his side.

She was so competent, Sarah. Catching Miss Priss before the cat landed on the marble tile and was hurt, despite the injury to her chin. Bianca would have let the cat fall before letting it near her precious face. Directing the situation without seeming to take control. Her kindness to Bella.

Franco couldn't reconcile her decency as a person with her dislike of him. *I can't get her out of my head.*

"When you call her, you can ask how her chin is."

Damn it. Bella heard him say he'd be calling. And once Bella had something in mind, she was tenacious.

"I'll remember. Now, how about a snack?"

"Oatmeal cookies?"

"You bet. Do you have homework?" It seemed ridiculous to him that a seven-year old had homework, but her teacher insisted it was important.

"Spelling." Bella stuck out her tongue. "I don't like spelling. I'd rather do math."

Franco laughed. "That's what we have spell check for on the computer, princess. I am not so good, either."

They walked into the apartment, Paisley dashing for her water dish. The puppy had healed very nicely, and none of the other pups in the batch were affected. Unlike what Sarah might believe, he would never sell damaged goods.

That wasn't how you got return customers, or more importantly, built a good reputation. After the fiasco with Bianca, he didn't want his daughter tainted by any more negativity.

"Why don't you go change out of your school uniform, and I'll get the mixing bowls out."

"Okay, Daddy. Maybe you should call Sarah?"

Like a bull dog, with a bone clamped in its teeth. "Later."

He wished he hadn't said anything. But that woman got under his skin like a tick. Annoying. Demeaning. And dangerous.

Perhaps if he got Bella involved with the cookies, she'd forget.

He wanted to forget all about Sarah Murphy himself.

Chapter Four

A half hour later, Sarah had deposited the check into her bank account, put a bandage over the gouge in her chin, and raced toward the little Publix on the corner to get the baking supplies. One recipe called for peanut butter, which might be interesting, and the thought of Benny with a mouthful made her laugh. Sarah definitely wanted to try some pumpkin, which was supposed to help with canine digestion issues.

She grabbed a red basket by the front door and quickly headed toward aisle 5.

"Sarah!"

She turned around at the sound of a young girl's voice, and sure enough, there was Bella standing near the baking supplies. Of course, Franco was there, too. Lean and sophisticated, a male model artfully lost among the sugar. Just hanging out with Betty Crocker.

"Hi!" Sarah smiled at Bella, who clutched a bag of chocolate chips in one hand and butterscotch in the other—she couldn't be any cuter, purple shorts and all. She didn't let her gaze settle on Bella's father as she said slowly, "Mr. de Silva."

Franco flinched and folded his hands behind his back. He'd changed from his black polo to a fitted black t-shirt, more casual but he still emanated money. Class.

Bella ran over and showed her choices to Sarah. "What do you like best? Chocolate?"

It was obvious from the way that Bella only lifted the bag of chocolate which one was her favorite.

"Chocolate?" Sarah guessed.

"Yes!" She ran back and put the butterscotch on the shelf. "See, Daddy? Chocolate is the best."

Sarah, feeling awkward and ungainly in her work uniform with the bandage on her chin, searched the shelves for what she wanted, though she was having a hard time concentrating. She felt Franco's animosity from fifty paces.

"Are you making cookies?" Bella asked, hooking one arm around her dad's leg, the bag of chocolate chips in her opposite hand.

Franco maintained a polite smile that suggested Sarah run off a short dock into an empty lake.

"Sort of." She kept her attention on Bella. "For my dogs."

"Cookies for dogs?" Bella laughed with delight.

"And I thought you were spoiled, Bella," Franco drawled.

"It's not that," Sarah clarified. "It's just that most of the ingredients in the dog treats aren't really good for them, so," she let her sentence trail off. Now was not the time to preach from her soap box.

Franco smiled with less vehemence. "They sell healthy treats."

"But they cost a fortune," she said. "And the shelter is on a tight budget." *Uncomfortably tight.*

"Do you cook?" Franco asked. "For your family?"

Being the target of his intense focus unnerved her and she tightened her grip on the handheld basket. "No family. As far as cooking, I know the basics."

His clipped nod seemed to say he wasn't the least bit surprised that she was single and a disaster in the kitchen.

"Yet you expect to make tasty treats?"

The bandage on her chin itched. Nothing she did around this man was graceful or elegant. She felt like the bull in the de Silva china shop. "Yes. I'm going to try, anyway." Determination had gotten her through college, and given her the opportunity to start her own business.

So what if she tripped over her own feet around this man? He was nothing to her, in the scheme of things, but a thorn in her side. He probably had enough money to buy her warehouse ten times over.

"Can Paisley have one? She likes treats. But she can only have a little bit, because she is a little dog. Dr. Wilton said so."

"Sure. I'll give some to Paisley. After Pippa and Benny try them out and make sure they taste good."

"Pippa and Benny?" Bella shifted from hanging on to her dad's left leg to his right.

"Those are my dogs. I also have a one-eyed cat. And the animals for adoption, of course. That number fluctuates." She scanned the shelves for rye, and got some whole wheat flour too.

"What does that mean?" Bella asked.

"Goes up and down." Sarah regretted the phrase immediately and refused to look anywhere near Franco. She felt the heat inch up her throat.

"Oh." Silence thrummed along the aisle, then, "Can I come and see your dogs?"

Franco coughed into his fist. "Come on Bella, let's go home and finish our cookies. People cookies."

"We ran out of oats," Bella told Sarah. "And we needed chocolate chips."

"I've never had oatmeal cookies with chocolate chips." Sarah looked over and saw that Bella's purple toenails perfectly matched her shorts. *When was the last time I painted my nails?*

"You should come and have some. With a big glass of milk. Does your chin hurt? Daddy was worried about it."

Sarah risked a glance at Franco, who wore his customary scowl. "You were? How sweet." She fought a chuckle.

"He was going to call you. My daddy thinks you're nice."

Laughing now, Sarah said, "Really?" She could only imagine the conversation the two of them must have had. "Bella, you are adorable. How about we trade treats for cookies once I figure out the recipe?"

"Yeah! Can we, Daddy?"

Franco was railroaded by his beautiful daughter. Sarah actually felt sorry for the poor guy—a teensy bit. Uh, Mr. de Silva.

"Of course." He took Bella by the hand and headed toward the cash register to check out. "It sounds like we will be seeing each other again," he said, his face expressionless.

He didn't sound happy about it, and for some reason, that made Sarah smile. "Bye!"

Franco and Bella walked the two blocks home. He preferred an active lifestyle, an important part of staying fit while eating the foods he enjoyed. He'd skied in Vale, dived the Australian reef, sailed the Caribbean. Snow-shoed, parasailed, he loved it all. He'd even gone on safari in Africa. Nothing scared him.

Until raising Bella.

There were so many ways he could screw things up. One wrong step off of the curb, and she could break a leg. One look away in the supermarket, and she could be kidnapped. If he wasn't vigilant, something terrible might happen.

He had no control.

It was humbling for a man of his position to be brought so low.

"It says to cross, Daddy," Bella said, tugging on his hand. "Cookies, cookies. I can be the Cookie Monster and eat all of the cookies. You wouldn't get any."

"You would not share with your *papai*?" He shook his head as she skipped the last few steps to the opposite side of the street, swinging his hand. "That is not very kind."

"All right," Bella said. "I will give you one. And Bob one, and Sarah one. Can Paisley have one?"

"Chocolate is not okay for dogs, princess. It could hurt them very bad. Never give Paisley chocolate, all right?"

She nodded, her eyes wide. Bella was such a mix between he and Bianca and every once in a while she gave him a look reminiscent of her mother. Bella was sweeter, innocent. Bianca had been conniving, though he'd been infatuated with her despite it. He'd never planned on children. He'd enjoyed his lifestyle. He could handle a bitch of a wife—she entertained him, and gave him his freedom.

Now he knew why. She had other things to do when he wasn't looking.

After the funeral, friends came forward with stories of her wild parties and crazy antics. Did they think this would comfort him? Or his daughter?

"I won't ever give Paisley chocolate. I promise." She held up her pinky. "Pinky swear."

"What?" *What was she talking about?*

"Hold out your pinky, Daddy. We have to swear on it. Kennedy, she's my friend at school, she showed me how to do it. It means you promise the bestest, most serious promise you can."

Baffled, he curled his pinky around his daughter's and gave it a shake. *Americans.*

They went into the condo, the cool air a rush of relief from the sun. "Hello, Bob," Franco said.

Bella released his hand and raced for the elevators. "Hi Bob!" She pushed the button on the gleaming gold panel. "We are making cookies. Want one?"

"I would never turn down a homemade cookie, young lady," Bob said, sharing a grin with Franco. "All that energy, even after the walk. If I could bottle that up and sell it? I'd have my own penthouse."

Franco chuckled. "She keeps me running, that's for sure."

He got into the elevator. Bella pushed the button to the top floor. Franco owned this condo prior to marrying Bianca. He'd invested in several properties during the recession and still owned a few along the Gold Coast. The lovely Bianca had decided she'd wanted him, for whatever reason, and pursued him. At almost thirty, marriage was the only thing he hadn't tried, so he didn't fight too hard.

As a personal chef to the stars, he knew many of the same people as Bianca. After three years, the marriage was stagnating. Franco told himself he would have stayed, but he'd never know if that was true or not since Bianca got pregnant.

"We're home," Bella sing-songed, skipping out of the elevator.

"We sure are, princess."

He'd sold everything in Brazil, ended all ties with their life there. They would never go hungry, but that wasn't enough. Bianca once had complained of feeling empty, worthless. A beautiful shell.

He never wanted Bella to feel that way. It was why he needed to create a community for her here. His parents, killed in a sea plane accident on the Amazon, had been a constant in his life. They'd grounded him in what mattered.

Being in service in some way to others. Donating back for the good of all.

He'd never minded working, for pay, at the homes of Bianca's peers—it was his career. His passion. She'd said a few times that she found it demeaning. When she'd been drunk, stoned. *Lost.*

"Daddy, you are not listening to me," Bella said in a serious tone. She'd crossed her arms and waited for him to look at her.

He laughed, refusing to go down the rabbit hole that had been his deceased wife's life. "You are right. My apologies. What were you saying?"

She dropped her arms and ran over to bury her face against his knees. "You looked sad. I don't want you to be sad. I mean it," she added sternly.

"I'm sorry, sweetheart. Sometimes…"

"Were you thinking of Mama?" The question came in a whisper. They rarely talked about Bianca.

He didn't want to lie. No dwelling in despair, but the therapists had encouraged him to be honest about his feelings. "Yes."

"Do you miss her?" Bella tightened her grip around his legs.

God, no. "I love you, Bella." He dropped down to his knees so that he was nose to nose with his daughter. "Do *you* miss her?"

She shrugged, her mouth unsmiling. "She could be mean." As if not to speak ill of the dead, Bella quickly added, "But she smelled like flowers, the white ones that bloomed in the backyard. She was beautiful."

"Yes, she was. But maybe not so much on the inside." His eyes welled as he realized how much damage Bianca had done. "You are beautiful on the inside and the outside, and that is much more important." He tugged on her waist-length curls, but then covered her heart with his hand.

"People can't see what's on the inside," Bella said with a frown.

"It is important to take the time to look beyond noses and mouths and hair." Franco bowed his head, ashamed of the plastic world he'd left behind. "What matters is someone's heart." He wiped his eyes with the back of his hand. "*Anjinho*, my little angel, you are only seven, but you are smart and caring." Franco got to his feet before he lost complete control. There was sharing, and falling apart. Two different animals and he wasn't going there in front of his child. "And you deserve oatmeal and chocolate chip cookies. I can't wait to try them."

"You really think it's a good idea?" Bella scampered to the barstool and the high-top counter.

"Creative minds always think outside of the box. Sometimes it tastes good, sometimes," he shrugged. "You have to try again. The point being, Bella, is that you have to try."

He bowed his head. There were so many ways he could mess this parenthood thing up, but his daughter would know he loved her. As to the rest? *I'm doing the best I can.*

Chapter Five

The kitchen timer dinged and Sarah, oven mitts she'd bought at the dollar store on each hand, took another tray of bone-shaped treats from the oven. She set them on the stove top and winced. Burned.

Martin scooted his chair back from the small round kitchen table and peered toward the pan. "A little *too done* this time, perhaps?"

She cursed under breath. The last two batches had been gooey so she'd adjusted the time. Pippa and Benny waited expectantly by the table, ears perked. "They love my cooking," she said, eyeing the mess.

"They eat from the garbage."

"Whatever." Tears threatened, but Sarah held them at bay. "The recipe said to spray the pan, and I did that. They shouldn't stick." She'd followed the directions exactly.

"Honey, you're cooking with rye. That's nasty, no matter what you add to it. It made those poor girls in Salem act like witches."

"That's simplifying a bit, don't you think?" Sarah tried to lift the treats free of the pan, but they broke. Benny stood up on his hind legs, still willing to give it a taste. Pippa sat back, waiting to see what would happen to Benny first. *Smart girl.*

Martin stirred another sugar packet into his herbal tea. "Speaking of witches, don't forget I have to visit my grandmother this Sunday."

Sarah leaned her head back. They had a booth at the Farmer's Market that Martin usually manned. "I forgot."

"Call your mama, she loves to help you." Martin sipped, made a face, then ripped open another sugar packet. Sarah looked at the three discarded wrappers on the table, realizing that he had four more to go before he had it just right. But he never wanted to admit to liking seven sugars from the get-go. Claimed he didn't have a sweet tooth.

"I will." Sarah took off one oven mitt. "It's just that last time she came to help, she didn't want to leave."

"So give her a little chore to do. Make her happy. With your dad gone…" he shrugged. "She is probably lonely."

"My mother isn't lonely. Dad left a long time ago. She has a job she loves, and friends she meets for lunches on the weekend. Yoga. You name it, she's doing it. Why do you think I hired you, and fired her?"

"It was not the best financial decision," he observed, on packet number six. "She worked for free."

"I didn't want her to take on *my* job. She was starting to worry over the roof, and the bills and the cost of dog food."

"*Si*, I worry about this too."

"But I don't have holiday dinners with you. You don't feel I owe you just for breathing."

"Neither does your mama," Martin chided. "Jennifer loves you."

Sarah's shoulders heaved with daughter-guilt. "I know. But seriously? She was getting hives from worry. She told me she was allergic to the bunny, but she got a rash right after looking up the cost of rabbit pellets."

Martin sipped his tea and sighed with pleasure. "Delicious. And so healthy. You should have some, Sarah. You're working too hard."

"Don't start." She held up the oven mitt like a stop sign.

"*Ai!* All right, I'll mind my own business."

"My mother would never say that. She'd get her

feelings hurt."

"I think we can both agree that I am not your mother." He looked over his nose and fluttered his eyelashes.

Sarah burst out laughing, imagining her mother masquerading as Diana Ross. "Thank you for that." She blew on the treats, cooling the edges enough to give each of the dogs a taste.

Benny sniffed, eyed her in question, but then gingerly took it in his mouth. He sat down, licked it a few times, then swallowed. Pippa sniffed, backed up a step, and looked at Benny. Benny made to take hers, so she barked once then downed the pumpkin and rye blob.

Sarah put the tray on the table and attacked the hard treats with a spatula. "Want one?"

"Are you joking?" Martin asked.

"What?" She took a piece and nibbled. "They aren't bad. This is pumpkin. Full of fiber."

Martin arched his brow, then accepted a broken section. He sniffed, dunked it in his tea, and swallowed. "Mmm." His mouth twisted.

"I did some research. Dogs have taste buds. They can prefer sweet over savory." Sarah looked down at Benny, who sat within tossing reach. "Benny likes fruit, which gave me the idea for the Berrylicious Biscuit."

"Oh, my, you're naming them already?"

"Why not? Pippa likes savory. I'm planning on a BacoBurger."

Martin nodded, getting into the spirit. "If these are good, we can add them to the website. People might buy them if we put them in a cute box."

"I don't know..." Sarah stared at the tray of funky treats. Would customers pay for them, once she perfected the recipe? She hadn't thought beyond wanting something decent and affordable for her own animals.

"It would be a way to add money to our empty coffers," Martin said.

She thought about Mrs. Drummel. She had money, and she'd wanted to spend it on Miss Priss/Jasmine. Hope fluttered in her belly. "If customers want the best for their pet, why shouldn't we offer it?"

"I agree—in theory." Martin picked up another square and nibbled. "But honey, this isn't the best. As not-your-mother, I can be honest with you. But there's potential."

"I'm working on it." Sarah propped her elbows on the table. "I'll get it right if it takes me a dozen batches."

"Also, not to be a rain cloud on your parade, but I think there might be rules before we start selling them." Martin settled back in his chair. "Licensing. I can look it up for you."

"Don't worry about it," Sarah quickly decided. "I can't afford any more business ideas unless they pay. Now listen, since we're talking hard facts here, we need to discuss the roof."

He took a fortifying sip of his tea. "Go."

"I have one quarter of what I need for the roof. And that's with my cousins giving me a contracting deal. They've offered to do the labor for next to nothing if I can just buy the supplies."

"Are they single, these cousins of yours?" Martin asked with interest.

"Single and straight. Pay attention!" She tapped the space between them. "What if we have a fundraiser?"

"To get money for the roof? In a month?"

"Why not? We work in a very lucrative place. I'm sure that if people knew we were under the gun, they'd help."

"Rich people want more for their money, Sarah," Martin said. "They're rich 'cause they don't spend it."

She crossed her legs at the ankles. Nashville swiped at her bootlace. "I've been realizing that. Though Mrs. Drummel paid extra today."

"She owed it to you for being such a diva. What about Franco de Silva? Want me to ask him for a donation? Or we could do a car wash!"

"No car wash." She shuddered, images of high school fundraisers making her slightly sick. Maybe it was the dog treats. "I've got a call into my friend Courtney to see if she has any ideas for a higher-end dinner or something. And leave Franco alone. I have enough on my plate without adding an egomaniac." A very wealthy, very good-looking egomaniac.

"You're blushing," Martin teased. "You think he is

gorgeous too."

Sarah couldn't lie, so she kept her mouth shut.

"You like him?" He smacked her wrist with a twisted napkin.

"No." There were so many things she didn't like about Franco. Yet he did crazy things to her heart rate. "Of course not." She didn't really know him.

"I think you do. When was the last time you went on a date?"

"That is none of your business!" She tried to free another treat but it was glued to the pan. Had it been since she broke things off with her fiancé?

"I've known you for almost a year now and not once have I seen you so much as flirt with a customer."

"They're animals. It's against the law." Sarah uncapped a bottle of water and drank half in one go. Franco's handsome face wouldn't leave her mind. His full lower lip, his smooth-shaven jaw.

"You know what I mean," Martin said, gesturing toward the heavens with a flourishing hand. "You work your fingers to the bone. Let me see your nails. Manicure? Ha!"

"I don't just work. I swim, or hang out at the pier. Paddle board. None of those things require that I paint my nails."

"You are an attractive woman."

Sarah snorted. She compared herself to the type of woman that Franco might date and her confidence slipped. He probably had super models calling him all the time.

"What? See what I mean? You have forgotten your femininity!"

"I have not." Oh no. *Was he right?* He was right. "I don't see the point..."

"To get a date. To dance and have drinks and make love under the moon light."

Making love?

Martin got up, took her hand and pulled her to her feet. He swung her out, and twirled her back in. "You've got good hips. Made for dancing." He hiked his brows suggestively. "And other things."

Embarrassed, Sarah yanked from Martin's grip—which was stronger than it looked. "I don't dance." She walked around the table to the sink and started the hot water running. If she didn't soak the bowls they'd be ruined. "I'm not that kind of girl. Even in high school I knew that I wanted to work with animals, so I volunteered at the local zoo. I didn't really go to parties." The kids her own age seemed way too young, wanting to drink and get high when she preferred studying with her dog on the beach.

Martin turned the water off. "We can clean up later. Sarah, you have too much to offer to be alone."

"I'm not alone." She twisted the faucet back on and gave Martin a raised brow. "I was engaged, you know."

"You were?" Martin leaned against the counter and

watched her wash dishes, reaching down for a dry towel from the drawer behind him. "It is too painful to talk about?"

"No. I broke up with him. He was the vet I interned with. I was his assistant before I decided that I wanted to save unwanted pets, not stitch them up." She rinsed and handed him the bowl.

He dried it and put it in the strainer on the counter. "Sounds like a good match. What happened?"

"We both cared about the well-being of animals. But my passion is rescuing them, which he thought was a waste of time and talent." Sarah smacked the counter. "And money."

"He didn't support you?" Martin sighed with disappointment.

"He wanted to control "us" as a partnership, and I, silly me, thought I should be an equal member of our relationship. I loved him, but I couldn't stay."

"Men can be such idiots."

Sarah laughed and rinsed the last dish, stacking it on top of the other bowls. "He thought I was a fool for leaving. I need a man that realizes I can make my own decisions, mistakes and all. A man who understands I don't need rescuing. Until then, I am happy with who I am."

He held up his hands. "You will find him, Sarah. Stay strong. Speaking of strong women, Diana calls." Martin fluttered his lashes provocatively. "That Diva used every ounce of her sensuality to entice."

"I'm not like that, Martin."

"You have your own Sarah-ness that is very sexy. You should let her out to play once in a while." He made a growling sound in his throat and walked out the door.

The man knew how to make an exit.

For reasons she didn't want to over-evaluate, Franco remained front and center in her head. He wasn't the sort of man she usually found attractive. He exuded masculinity, disrupting her balance. He'd had her subconscious in knots trying to mesh the arrogant shop owner with the caring single dad.

Sexy? Definitely?

Full of himself? Yes. So not her style.

Her mind couldn't get beyond how gorgeous he'd been, standing in the baking aisle, staring at her as she helped Bella choose between chocolate and butterscotch. *Mr. de Silva to you.*

Cheeks hot at the memory of his set-down, Sarah doubted he'd be asking her out on a date anytime soon. Who was she kidding, giving him a starring role in her fantasies?

Laughing at herself, she danced around the kitchen table, the dogs at her heels. The phone rang and she waltzed toward the desk. "Pet Rescue, how may we help you today?" She sank into the chair and rolled a few inches back.

"Sarah? This is Franco de Silva."

Fun and games came to a halt. Her heart thumped in her chest. Painfully. "Yes? How may I help you?" *Well, that couldn't have sounded stuffier.*

"Bella and I are wondering if you'd like a cookie?"

Sarah could just imagine Bella tugging at her dad's arm until she got her way. It would be very mean to keep him hanging. "Sure." *Be friendly, Sarah.*

"We can drop them by. Bella wants to see your animals."

And does Dad do everything Bella wants? She sat up straighter in the chair. She had no business judging how anybody reared their kid. At least he was sticking around, which was more than her dad did. "All right. When would be a good time?" *Next week? Next year?*

"We're here now. In the parking lot."

"Oh," Sarah squeaked. She looked up as the door opened, the chime over the top alerting her to their arrival. "Come in." She hung up the phone. *Well, hell.*

Franco rather enjoyed the flash of panic as it crossed Sarah's usually calm face. He took in the soft beige foyer of the facility. Books on pet ownership lined waist-high shelves. Brochures sat on the top, next to a few framed photos of various animals and owners. Satisfied customers, maybe?

Light brown tile led to an open area to the right,

where Sarah had her desk and chair, creating an office space. A kitchen was behind that in the farthest corner. A large door next to the shelves was closed and he wondered if that was where the animals were kept. Was it a garage?

A cat sat on a cushion in the window, but didn't give him the time of day. Two small dogs raced around the desk, avoiding Bella as she chased them. *Giggling.*

He sniffed. "Smells like pumpkin," he said. Burned pumpkin, to be exact.

Sarah stayed in her chair—something with wheels that could be gotten from any office supply store. A large blue dog bed was at the corner of the faux-oak desk. "Sit, Benny. Good girl, Pippa. Hi, Bella."

"Hi!"

"They won't bite?" he asked.

Lifting her head with obvious annoyance, Sarah answered, "Not unless Bella bites them first."

Bella laughed and plopped down on the floor, cross-legged, as the dogs scrambled to the bed with nervous barks. "I won't," she said.

Franco shouldn't care that Sarah's tanned knees poked below her khaki shorts, or that her calves were nicely shaped.

He shouldn't notice that her blonde hair, usually in a tight serviceable ponytail, had come loose, sending tendrils around her face to soften the sharp planes of her cheekbones.

Or that the way she filled out her navy blue polo let

him know she had curves to go with her no-nonsense attitude.

He appreciated her kindness, touching Bella's shoulder, petting her dogs so they felt safe as his daughter enthusiastically (and not so gently) scratched their ears.

But he didn't want to. He was in the enemy camp and it was hard to let go of his anger toward her, knowing that she had it in for him. Listening to Bella's laughter reinforced why he was here. His daughter's happiness meant everything to him, and if it meant riding out this liking she had for Sarah, then so be it.

The faster he could get out of here, the better.

Franco followed the smell of burned pumpkin. The kitchen area was tiny, with just enough room for a circular table, three chairs, sink, refrigerator and stove. Nothing like his state-of-the art kitchen in the condo.

A cooking tray with burned and broken bone-shaped cookies was in the center of the table.

He leaned down and sniffed. Molasses?

"Uh, those didn't come out well," Sarah called, getting up from her office chair. Bella and the dogs got up too.

"I see that." He studied the tray. "Didn't you use a cooking spray?"

"Of course I did." Cheeks crimson, she pointed to the can next to the stove.

"What is in them?" He had the idea that Sarah was too busy "saving the world" to spend much time in the kitchen.

She bristled, jamming her hands into her pockets. "Chicken stock. Molasses. Rye. I followed the directions. I must have done something wrong."

Bella scooted up to the table to peer at the tray. "Do they taste good?"

"No. I tried them." Sarah scrunched her nose. "Too dry. The rye is bitter. Even Benny didn't like them."

"Which one is Benny?" Bella asked.

"The Chihuahua." Sarah leaned over and tugged at his wagging tail.

"A dog with discerning tastes," Franco decided, looking down at the mostly brown-eyed dog. Cataracts. Old. But sweet-tempered, for a rat chaser.

"I like Pippa," Bella declared, picking up the black toy Pomeranian. "She's pretty."

"She just likes food, really, so she isn't much fun," Sarah said somewhat apologetically. "But if you have a tasty treat? I'm pretty sure she could learn any trick in the world."

Pippa strained toward the tray, her small pink tongue dangling to the right as her bead-like black eyes focused on the pumpkin bones.

"Nothing the matter with knowing what you want," he said. The dog was like her owner. He sensed that Sarah, too, went after what she wanted.

"You don't like them," Sarah reminded the dog.

Pippa barked in protest, never taking her eyes from

the tray.

Bella put her down and Pippa wobbled away, but not too far from the action.

"What's the matter with her leg?" Franco asked.

"Bad hips. Surgery gone wrong. But at the end of the day?" She speared him with a hard, green stare. "Puppy mill. Over-breeding for a beautiful face. Genetically, she's a mess."

"Was she a rescue?" He leaned against the spindle-back chair.

"From the puppy store you bought and took over." She tensed.

"Ah." Well, that somewhat explained her anger. "I don't operate that way. Dr. Wilton approves every animal we have for sale."

"Really?" Sarah relaxed and nodded at him. "The previous owners didn't care at all. They just wanted something flashy. Expensive."

"And so you closed the shop?"

She crossed her arms. "Yup. It took me six months to prove what they were doing. But I did it—we caught the people who were breeding the puppies and selling them with false papers, too. They made a bundle, taking advantage of the tourists."

"And you just assumed that I was going to pick up where they left off?"

"How should I know what you're planning?"

He liked that she stood up for what she believed in,

but she had no reason to distrust him. Other than that bucket of mop water during the first week he'd been open, he'd done nothing wrong.

"Daddy, are you mad?" Bella pulled at his fingers.

"Not at you, princess." He was mad that there were people willing to do anything for a dollar, but that wasn't a conversation for right now. He supposed that if their roles were reversed, he would be just as vigilant as Sarah.

"I'm sorry," Sarah said, touching his arm. "I'm not being a very good host. Would you like some juice? I have carrot, apple and berry."

"You have carrot juice?" Bella wrinkled her nose.

"It's actually very good," Sarah said, chuckling. "Want to try? Or would you prefer something else? I also have bottled water, or I can make coffee."

She said the last to him, but he was more interested in trying her juices. "I'll taste the carrot. What do you use to sweeten it?"

"Honey. Locally harvested."

Probably a hard-core vegan. Save the planet, save the world. So not his type, and a bore at cocktail parties. "Are you a vegetarian then?"

"No!" She laughed with surprise, the sound natural. He'd bet she'd never spent any time being anybody other than herself. "I'm not that healthy, really, but I don't always eat regularly so if I make these juices ahead of time, I know I'm getting some vitamins with my cheeseburger."

"Glad to hear you're a meat eater." Would she

appreciate his cooking? He was good at it. *Why do I care?*

Bella piped up. "I like veal and steak and chicken marsala and,"

"I'm raising a carnivore too," he said, his stomach tensing. Why should imagining Sarah tearing into a t-bone get his blood simmering? "In Brazil we have *churrasco*, which is barbecue meat, sometimes skewered on a sword."

Sarah tossed her head and laughed. "What else do you eat? Does everything come with a weapon?"

"The national dish is beans, pork and beef. *Feijoada.* Like a stew. Just a spoon, and some crusty bread for scooping." Maybe she'd like his *milanesas*, tender breaded steak, served with duck ragu?

God, what was he thinking? It was time to get home before he did something stupid like offer to cook for her and no matter how much he loved Bella, he was not making Sarah a meal.

"My dad is the best chef," Bella said. "Maybe he can help you with your dog treats, Sarah. Can you, Daddy?"

"Nothing nasty in here?" he asked again, meeting her eyes and lifting the end of the tray. Was it warped?

She tucked strands of hair behind her ear and shook her head. "Four ingredients. Rye, pumpkin, chicken stock. Molasses. And the spray oil that was supposed to keep them from sticking."

He reached out and broke off a piece, putting the smallest bit on the tip of his tongue. Part of his success was his amazing palate, which he'd gotten from his mother and his grandmother. "Hmm. Have you tried honey for sweetness instead of the molasses? Maybe cut the rye with wheat flour, for a softer biscuit. I'd suggest garlic, for savory, but I read somewhere that it's bad for dogs."

"Garlic?" Sarah repeated it as a question. She got three glasses from the cupboard and took a pitcher of orange-colored juice from the refrigerator. "I worked with a vet and he suggested garlic—we're talking a pinch—added to food to keep away fleas, ticks and mosquitoes."

Franco opened the cupboard, looking for spices. "Very interesting. Herbal flea control and no vampires."

Sarah's smile lit her face. "I never would have pegged you as believing in vampires."

"Vampires are just pretend." Bella drank some of her juice and licked her upper lip. "This is yummy."

"I'm glad you like it." Sarah squeezed his daughter's shoulder and then turned her bright gaze toward him. "Well? What's the verdict? Should I give up, or try again?"

"Daddy says you always have to try." Bella put her glass on the table.

Sarah leaned against the counter, juice in hand. "Your daddy sounds like a pretty smart guy." She addressed Bella but then lifted her eyes to his as if offering a possible truce.

Franco cleared his throat. "I have the occasional

good idea. With Bella to keep me in line, how can I go wrong?" He glanced at the clock on the plain white stove. "4 o'clock already? Come on, Bella. We should get going." Now that he knew where Sarah worked, he could stop wondering about her. About what she did when she wasn't harassing him. That would be good.

"My daddy makes the best steak. I already did my homework." Bella skipped across the room after Nashville, who did her best to avoid the little girl's eager embrace. "Sarah, can you come to dinner tonight?"

Hell, no. Franco ground down on his back teeth before the words actually left his mouth. He wished he could haul his daughter out of the shop, take back her innocent invitation, stop her attachment to Sarah before it went any further.

"I," Sarah hedged, raising a confused expression his way. In fact, the sudden drop of color beneath her tan let him know she was uncomfortable, too. "Mr. de Silva?"

"Franco, please." So, he'd been an ass. She brought out the worst in him. When he thought about expanding Bella's community, it was with people who didn't make him think about sex. Or his lack of having sex. Like Bob, or Dr. Wilton.

He didn't want to care about anybody else in an intimate way.

"I don't know..." Sarah said, looking uncertain.

"Why not?" he asked, his gut clenched as if hovering over a twenty-foot drop off. "I make a mean t-bone, and we've got an amazing view." No way would she agree. They had nothing in common.

"I'm sure," she said with a repressed smile that made him wonder if she was laughing at him. "Nothing but the best, if I recall."

He winced. He hadn't been much of a gentleman.

"Come, Sarah, come! Please?" Bella put her hand in Sarah's. "I'll show you my room."

Franco immediately pictured Sarah in his bedroom. With a glass of wine. Candles. In khaki shorts? He shook the thought from his mind.

"Okay," Sarah said. "You've tasted my cooking, now I'll get to taste yours. What time?"

Chapter Six

Sarah pinched her wrist, still not quite believing she'd agreed to have dinner in the penthouse with Franco de Silva, her sworn enemy, and his adorable, motherless daughter. God, she couldn't even afford to bring a decent bottle of wine. Maybe a six pack of dark beer. Guinness went well with beef. Right?

They'd stood awkwardly after she'd said yes, she sliding her eyes away first. What was he thinking? She couldn't tell, but she imagined there was some regret hidden behind his neutral expression. Bella rescued the moment by bringing a surprisingly calm Nashville to show her dad.

"Look, Daddy. One eye! But she can still see with the other one."

"Amazing." Franco pushed away from the counter and said, "We should probably get going if we're making dinner. You're helping, yes, Bella?"

"Yeah!" She released the cat, who shook herself and stuck her tail straight in the air, stalking beneath the relative safety of the table to hide.

"Seven thirty, is that too late?" he asked. His voice was calm. Cool. No big deal.

"Perfect." It would give her time to find a damn dress. This was Martin's fault for putting the idea of being a woman in her head. But this was not a date. This was a set up from his daughter, who sweetly thought of Sarah as a friend.

"We didn't see the bunny! Do you still have the bunny?"

"We do." Sarah stuck her hands in her pockets and looked at Franco. "The animals are housed back here. It won't take long. We've got kittens, an iguana, three dogs and a rabbit."

"You've rescued them all?" Franco's enigmatic expression might have been mocking her, it was hard to tell. She tended to wear her beliefs on her shirtsleeve, which could come off as obnoxious, according to her ex.

"Yes." She smiled, proud of her job whether or not

he understood her calling. "Follow me."

She led the way through the offices to the warehouse. Air conditioned, with high-set windows that allowed plenty of light, Sarah had separated the space with screens, fencing off areas so that the dogs had room to run. The iguana had his own heater in a corner, with a big branch she and Martin had fixed to the wall. She'd also brought in a lot of indoor plants, just to give the place an outdoor feel.

"This is very nice," Franco said, turning around to take it all in.

The sincere compliment made her nervous. "Thanks."

"Why is that section unused?" He pointed to the far rear corner.

"The roof is solid but it needs to be brought up to code. A freak windstorm brought a tree through. Right before I bought it, actually." She'd gotten a discount on the building, but with the caveat she get the roof fixed within six months. She'd already asked for one extension, and she was told that there would be no more. "I love our community here, but the roofs are all supposed to match. My patched corner is, according to the town manager, an eyesore."

Franco chuckled. "I didn't notice."

Bella raced around the area, her dark curls flying behind her like a cape. "She's really great," Sarah said.

Franco, his eyes on his daughter as she greeted the three mutts, agreed. "I am a very fortunate man."

Not a very egomaniac thing to say—or was it? "Listen, I don't have to come to dinner…"

"You've already agreed, Sarah. It would disappoint Bella if you changed your mind. You said yourself you don't take the time out for many proper meals. As a thank you for what you did for Paisley, I want to cook for you. Really." He took her hand and squeezed, making her palm itch.

"Okay." She slipped her hand free and clasped both of them behind her back. A thank you. That was nice. *Not a date.*

"Bella, it is time to go. Oh, no." Franco turned toward her, his brows drawn. "Did she give you the cookies we made?"

Sarah shook her head. "No."

"Bella!"

At his call, she came running, still grinning as if she was in Disneyland instead of a warehouse full of misfits. "Daddy?"

"Where are the cookies, honey?"

Her expression fell and she put her hand to her pocket. She pulled out a sandwich baggie, crushed, with a bow tied around the top. "Oops." Tears threatened.

Sarah reached for the plastic bag. "Not a big deal! How about we get a do-over? I try my recipe again, using honey for sweetener, and I'll bring them to your house. Hopefully you haven't eaten all of the cookies already?"

Bella shook her head, looking from Sarah to her

father. "We didn't, did we?"

"There are some in the container. What a good idea." He smiled at Sarah, his demeanor changing from uptight to genuine. For the first time, Sarah was the recipient of Franco's charm and her body trembled at the onslaught. "A do-over." He winked, the action inviting her into a conspiracy. "For all of us."

Mouth dry, Sarah ushered them out the front door, her emotions on high-alert. She was going to see Franco, for dinner. As a thank you for her services. An olive branch, to put the past behind them. Where to get a dress that fit her budget without looking cheap?

She picked up the phone, combining a portion of wheat flour to the rye, honey, pumpkin and chicken stock as she waited for her mother to pick up the phone. At the last minute she added a dollop of molasses.

"Hello, Sarah," her mom said. "Long time, no hear."

"Not the time for a guilt trip, Mom. I need two favors. I have to borrow a dress for tonight—it needs to look classy, but simple. And I really could use your help for the Farmer's Market on Sunday."

"Sure, sure," her mom readily agreed into the phone. "Why on earth do you need a dress? You haven't worn one since graduation. But I've got a silk sleeveless tunic style that will really match your eyes."

"You are a life-saver, Mom." She scraped the side of the bowl with the spatula.

"So? What's the occasion? Something for the

shelter?"

"No." Sarah said. "Well, sort of. Dinner with a client."

Silence. "Who?"

"Franco de Silva. The puppy store owner."

"But you closed them down!"

"The *new* puppy store owner. So far he's been on top of things."

"But you were certain he'd start right back up again, Sarah Murphy. You were in a bad mood for a month."

Moms. "Well, he seems to be following the rules."

"For now," her loyal mother huffed. "Better keep an eye on him. Maybe not the silk dress. I've got something less showy..."

"Mom!"

"How old is he?"

"I don't know. Thirty-five. Forty." *Gorgeous.* "He's got an adorable little girl. Bella."

"You can't date a man with kids."

"It's not a date!"

"Besides, you don't like kids."

"Says who?" Where did her mother get this stuff?

"You! No time, no desire. You swore on your thirtieth birthday that you didn't have a biological clock."

"I'm going to hang up now," Sarah said, setting the very well-mixed bowl of ingredients down on the counter with a thump.

"I just want you to be happy."

"Then loan me the dress. The green one. I'll pick it up on my way home from work, okay?"

Sarah punched the thick dough into shape, then rolled it into a flat, quarter-inch thick sheet. She took her bone-shaped cookie cutter and tried again. These had to turn out right. She was out of dough, out of pumpkin and out of patience.

She set the timer and quickly fed and walked the animals so she could leave early for a shower. Sarah held her breath when the timer went off, her stomach a knotted mess. Success? Or another waste of money she could ill afford...

Pippa and Benny followed her around the kitchen, staying just out of tripping range.

Opening the oven door, she was greeted with a nice pumpkin pie smell. "So far, so good," she said, setting the tray on the stove top.

"Golden brown, nothing burned." Her heart raced with anticipation. "If they taste good, we might have a winner!" Benny danced for all he was worth and Pippa spun herself round in circles until her tongue hung out.

Carefully lifting one of the corner treats, she breathed a sigh as it came up without crumbling. Solid, not too moist, but not like rock either. She broke off a corner and put it in her mouth. Franco had been right about the honey—it added just enough sweetness to get past the rye. Adding the flour gave it a nice texture. The tiny amount of molasses added a little spice.

"Ready guys?" Sarah turned to her taste-testers. "This is what you've been waiting for!" Benny gobbled his treat and raced around the table like a greyhound. Pippa swallowed, looking for more. Feeling very proud of herself, Sarah cleaned up the kitchen, got the dogs in the car, and went home to shower, a plastic container of treats for her mom's dogs, for her puppies, and for Bella's Paisley.

She was at her apartment in ten minutes, including her stop for Guinness. She'd decided to pick up the dress last so that she'd get less dog hair all over it.

Her mom, however, surprised her by dropping it off just as Sarah got out of the shower. Since she had a key, she'd let herself in and waited on the couch with Benny and Pippa.

"I'm here," her mom called once the shower turned off.

Sarah shot a panicked glance at the clock. It was seven already and she still had wet hair.

"Thanks, Mom." She walked out of the bathroom, down the hall to her living room. Her apartment was tiny, but cozy, and she liked the things she'd collected. Sea glass, driftwood, netting. Antique ship parts, like a brass bell and a captain's wheel, were part of her décor. She might work a lot, but the ocean was her home and spending time on the beach was her sanity.

"You smell nice," her mother said, getting up to kiss Sarah's cheek. "Sorry if I was too bossy, honey. I worry."

"I know." She looked her mom over. Blonde, curvy, cute in blue glasses and a cobalt dress. "You could have changed from work, Mom."

"Pah. We have to stick together. You know, Sarah, if things are too tight that you can move back home with me. I won't bother you, I swear."

"Things are not too tight." Her shoulders hitched. She wouldn't survive moving home.

"You have a bag of carrots in your refrigerator."

"Lazy shopping. Stop peeking!" Sarah looked around. "Where's the dress? Oh! I made dog treats from scratch."

"You made dog treats?"

"Yes," she said. Why was everybody so surprised she could operate an oven? "It took a few tries, seven, actually, to get it right, but here." Sarah handed over the plastic container she'd put together. "Taste."

Her mom sucked her lips in as if tucking them away. "Me? Don't you mean for Bert and Ernie?"

"Mostly, but I want you to try too. It won't hurt you."

As if it was on pain of death, her mother took a bite. Then smiled with pride. "Amazing! Sarah, these are great. The dogs will love them." She put the treat back in the container and closed the lid. "I hung both dresses up in your room, so you could choose."

"Thanks, Mom. If you don't mind letting yourself out? I'm running late."

"But!"

"No buts. If you stay, I'll second guess everything, and I just want to be myself."

Her mom scowled. "Fine. But you will look beautiful. How could you be anything else?"

~

Franco looked at the clock. 7:35. Maybe Sarah had talked herself out of coming. She couldn't miss the tension between them. What started out as anger had felt dangerously like something else. *Desire.* Part of him hoped she wouldn't come.

He scowled out the dining room window overlooking the ocean. Various shades of blue, from aqua to turquoise, shifted with each wave. The Atlantic Ocean soothed his soul like none other, and he'd been all around the world. Nothing was as beautiful as the Gold Coast of South Florida. Maybe he could take Bella snorkeling this weekend?

Get his mind off of a certain blonde save-the-world type who seemed to be under his skin. Bella would be disappointed that Sarah was a no-show, so ice cream at Sloan's might be in order.

"Sarah!" Bella squealed.

Sarah? How had she gotten up? Bob was supposed to buzz when they had company arrive. And while he'd been nursing his bruised ego, his daughter had probably sat on the intercom.

"Daddy, Sarah is here! She brought me a puppy!"

"What?" Not one of those mutts from her shelter? Not good.

"A stuffed animal," Sarah said with an easy laugh. He sucked in a breath at the sight of her, breezing into the kitchen with Bella leading and Paisley at her heels. "You should have seen your face just now."

Sarah Murphy was a knock out. At least, it seemed that way to his sucker-punched gut. Dressed in a silk sleeveless dress that teased her thighs, in a green that looked like sea glass, she shimmered with vibrancy. Her hair fell past her tanned shoulders in soft, loose waves that made her look like she'd just come from the beach.

"Do you surf?" he blurted.

"I try, but there's not much around here." She pointed out his window to the water below. "I snorkel, and dive. Paddle board. Do you like water sports?"

"Love them. Have you been kite boarding?"

"No, but it looks like so much fun, skimming the top of the ocean like you're flying!" Sarah handed over a six pack of Guinness. "My friend at the pier goes out all the time."

"Perfect," he said. "Dark beer is my favorite."

"I didn't know what else to bring," she confessed. She looked around the kitchen and dining room. "I mean, you have everything."

Not everything, he thought, opening them each a

beer. She was a ray of sunshine that he hadn't realized he'd missed.

"The steaks are marinating," he said. "Care for a seat?"

Bella climbed up to the barstool and pointed to the array of small dishes on the counter. "We made brie and crackers and some olives and everything that would prepare our pa..." She scrunched her nose. "Our *palate*, for our steak."

Sarah laughed easily and joined Bella at the bar. Franco wished she'd stayed next to him. She smelled fresh and he noticed the back of her hair was slightly damp. "Do you like to cook, too, Bella?"

"Daddy's teaching me. He used to cook for the girl with purple hair."

Franco smiled.

"Who?" Sarah asked.

"She's talking about Kelly Osbourne. Not a client, but I did cook for some famous people."

"Noooo!" Sarah said, reaching into her purse for a plastic container. "No way are these going to be good enough, then. Dang it. I thought I had a shot at impressing you."

Franco accepted the container. "Dog treats?"

"They're good," she said, popping an olive in her mouth.

He accepted her challenge, admiring her courage. Her sass. He took one and sniffed. Paisley waited patiently at his feet, while Bella clapped her hands. "I want to try!"

So Franco broke the treat into three parts, but he tasted it first. Pleasantly surprised. Then Bella, and finally Paisley.

"These are great, actually. Did you write down the amounts you used of everything so that you can recreate the recipe?"

Sarah's eyes sparkled. "Hmm. Sort of. I'm no doctor, but I have the handwriting of one. We'll see if I can decipher what I wrote tomorrow."

Bella said, "These are yummy, yummy. We get to have the oatmeal cookies for dessert!"

Franco heated the grill as the two ladies sat at the bar. He never felt self-conscious when cooking, but tonight he was very aware of his audience. He tossed his head back, getting his hair from his eyes without touching it.

"Can I help?" Sarah asked.

He liked her, he decided, uncertain if that was a good thing or a bad thing. "Nope. Bella and I made a salad, and rice with garlic and tomatoes. The meat is so tender it will only take ten minutes. I hope you brought your appetite."

Glancing up as he tossed the first steak on the sizzling grill, he met her gaze, which was just as hot. Just as sizzling. This was not khakis Sarah.

This Sarah met him on an elemental level and threatened to set his well-structured world off balance.

"I sure did," she said, lightly nibbling another olive

without releasing him from her spell.

Chapter Seven

Franco looked sexier than any television kitchen chef as he turned the savory steaks. Dark, waving hair loose around his chiseled face, his brown eyes almost black in the kitchen shadows.

She'd felt his interest heighten as he carefully checked her out. Not to be rude, but just, well, looking. Sometimes out of the corner of his eye, sometimes straight-on, with a smile.

It was nice. Too long since the last time she'd even cared about being thought attractive. She might not wear dresses, but she lived in bikinis during her time off so she had well-earned color from years in the sunshine.

"Smells wonderful," Sarah said. "The last time I had steak was on my birthday a few months ago. We went to Chatham House. I even ate lobster tail."

"How old are you, Sarah?" Bella asked, scooting her stool closer to Sarah.

"It is not polite to ask a lady her age, princess," Franco interjected.

"I'm thirty," Sarah answered. "Maybe it's okay if I ask how old you are?"

Bella nodded, her eyes serious. "Okay. I am seven. Daddy is thirty-eight." Her eyes widened. "Sorry, Daddy! Is that a secret?"

Franco laughed. "No secrets here. Obviously we couldn't keep one, anyway," he said to Sarah. "Come on, ladies. The table is set, the salad ready. Sarah, would you mind bringing the rice from the oven?"

A man in the kitchen was sexy, plain and simple. But this was not a date; this was a meal as a thank you from a grieving man and his daughter. Sarah had no business checking out his ass as he put the steaks on each of their plates.

But it was worth the peek. Jeans were made for this man's physique. Slim hips, lean waist, fitted t-shirt. She curled her fingers around the dish.

Setting the ceramic rice casserole on the trivet in the center of the table, she asked, "Here okay?"

"Perfect." His deep voice rumbled over her taut nerves.

He held out the chair for her to sit, politely scooting her in. "Thank you."

Sarah was pretty sure tension would get the better of her and she wouldn't be able to eat over this newly discovered attraction to a man way out of her dating pool. Not even in the same universe. His dining room table cost as much as her work truck.

Franco served Bella, and then Sarah, apologizing, "Sorry, I've just gotten used to dishing things out."

"It's fine," she said, kicking herself. What to talk about to be an interesting dinner companion? "Everything smells delicious. But then again, you've witnessed my culinary efforts."

"That last batch of dog treats was really terrific," he said with a wink. "And you make great juice."

Sarah put her napkin in her lap, thankful for the lessons in deportment her mother drilled into her head. Bread on the left, drinks on the right. Start with the outer fork first and move in from there.

These people lived daily in a world of luxury, whereas she was the occasional visitor. She didn't dwell on the comparison. Sarah truly loved the life she'd chosen for herself. She cut into her steak, took a bite and sighed. "I've never had anything this delicious. Never."

"Try it with a bite of rice," Franco said. "It's the marinade, of course, and the herbed butter. No dieting here!"

Bella's table manners were impeccable. Napkin in her lap, food cut into bite-sized pieces, no elbows to be found. "This is so good. But I'm full, Daddy. Can I be excused to watch cartoons?"

"You are trying to get extra television time because we have a guest," Franco declared.

Right on the money, going by Bella's crestfallen face. "Sorry, Sarah," she said.

"I am still eating, so I don't mind at all, if it's okay with your dad."

Bella switched her gaze toward her father, and Sarah watched him melt. "For half an hour. In English."

Bella, all smiles again, scampered away. "Thank you Daddy!" Paisley followed her as if fairly certain there would be crumbs.

"She has me wrapped around her finger," Franco said as she left, then shrugged and cut another piece of steak.

"English? She speaks so well. I can't believe it's thanks to watching cartoons." Sarah smiled, wondering if that system worked. Her cousin's kids were all addicted to Dora, and learned a little bit of Spanish along the way.

"We raised Bella bilingual, with an American nanny. Sometimes she likes to watch her cartoons in Spanish." He poured the rest of his beer into the glass.

"But you are from Brazil?" Sarah thought back to World History class. "You speak Portuguese?"

"Similar," he said, taking a drink. "Close enough for Bella when she feels homesick."

Sarah speared a piece of pink-in-the-center steak. The meat had been crusted with herbs before he'd grilled. "She's really cute. And right now? Easy to please," Sarah laughed. "Just wait until she wants a car." She bit off the end and chewed.

Franco didn't smile like she'd hoped. Instead, he nodded, meeting her eye to eye. "I don't want her to be a spoiled woman. Too much of everything ruined her mother."

Oh, hell. Sarah swallowed the steak stuck in her throat and quickly drank some of her beer. "I'm sorry." Dumb thing to say. "I mean, I don't know what happened in your past, but I'm sorry for the pain it caused—you and Bella. You both seem like you are doing all right."

His face hardened, then he shook his head and forced a smile. "We are. Bella and I love the ocean, so this was the first place I thought of when it was time to relocate. Bianca, her mother, my wife, was famous in Europe. She overdosed." Franco gritted his teeth. "Suicide. Bella discovered her mother in the bathtub, dressed in a black slip with a note clutched in her hand."

The food turned to sawdust in Sarah's mouth. "Poor Bella." *Poor Franco.* Why was he sharing this with her? Too much!

"I don't want to spoil my daughter, yet I can't help but worry over every step she takes. I can't protect her all of the time, and it keeps me up at night."

"You sound like my mother. Or any loving parent," Sarah said, responding to his very real pain by covering his hand with hers. "Were you not around, before the," she cleared her throat, "accident?"

"I traveled for my work, of course, and for pleasure. We had nannies for Bella, and when I was home, I spent time with her. Before I knew about Bianca's addictions. I thought I was leaving Bella in a loving mother's care. Instead, I placed my daughter in danger every time I left." He flipped his hand around so that their fingers entwined. "Bella could have been killed or kidnapped," his voice thickened as he went through what sounded to Sarah like a long list of self-guilt.

How terrible that he felt so bad. "She wasn't. Bella is sweet and kind. You are here now. You can't control everything. Actually," Sarah laughed softly, "there really isn't that much you can control. The basics. Food, lodging. You're giving her the best of everything. Yourself. But a freak tornado could wipe out the condo tomorrow. You can only live in the moment."

Franco released his grip, sliding his fingers to the edge of his plate. "I know that. Logically. But in my heart?" He glanced into the living room and the warm blue glare of the television playing cartoons. He smiled at Bella's laughter. "I love her."

"She is a lucky girl."

"I think it is the other way around." Franco seemed

to realize where the conversation had gone. "Sorry, it isn't often that I am around other grown-ups these days."

"It's all right." Sarah could be his friend. There was nothing taboo about making new friends, and in a friendship, money didn't matter. Franco needed a friend. She would not desire him, if he were her friend. Her mind called bullshit, but she'd deal with that later.

"Time to lighten the mood!" Franco got up and Sarah helped him clear the table. He piled the dishes in the sink, refusing to let her do them, or even rinse them off. "I have brandy and cigars," he said. "Dessert for the adults. On the balcony."

"Brandy?" She shook her head. "I've never had that before. And I don't smoke. At least not since the occasional cigarette in college."

"Cigars aren't really smoking. I'll show you." He reached across the cabinet, his chest brushing her arm, taking down two balloon-shaped glasses.

"I don't know."

"I swear you will like it." His eyes held hers captive as he practically pinned her to the counter. The attraction she kept denying flared to life.

"I should probably go," she said, her voice sounding breathless.

"You just got here." He brushed a strand of hair back from her cheek. Her skin buzzed as if she was already tipsy.

"I'm on call." Twenty-four hours a day. Did he feel

what she did?

"One small tiny taste." Glasses in hand, he remained in her space, so close she felt the heat off his body. She could count his eyelashes as he looked down at her, his gaze daring her to step outside her comfort zone.

"Teeny tiny," she finally agreed.

He nudged her forward with his hip. "Beyond the table. Bella, we will be on the balcony."

"All right, Daddy!"

"She's getting away with extra because you are here," Franco said. "She likes you very much."

"She's awesome." Sarah stepped out into the warm evening air coming off the ocean, and sank into a cushy outdoor sofa with a crazy panoramic view. "I never get tired of this." The sound of the waves was hypnotic.

"The ocean?" Franco sat down next to her, making her catch her breath.

"Yeah." She couldn't think of anything witty to say and knew if she tried she'd trip over her tongue.

"Are you from here? Ft. Lauderdale?" Franco asked, pouring from a clear bottle with a dark label.

"I am," Sarah said, accepting a small glass of amber liquid. She sniffed. "It smells fruity, sort of."

"Take a sip and let it sit on your tongue for a few seconds. See what else you can pick out." He raised his glass to hers and clinked. "I was raised in the mountains, but we spent summers on the water. Then I moved to Bahia, Salvador. That is where we had Bella. Well?"

Sarah didn't care for the sharp tang of alcohol, which seemed overwhelming at first. But she'd agreed to try, so she let the flavors sit.

"Oak? Berries. It's smoky."

"Good job," Franco said with approval. "Brandy is distilled wine—this particular brandy has been distilled in an oak keg for flavor. Here, try this now." He passed over a slim cigar, clipping and lighting the opposite end.

Sarah giggled nervously. "I, uh. Hmm."

"Do not inhale," he instructed, his brown eyes soft as velvet. Strong brows, thick lashes. She could get drunk on him and to hell with the brandy.

She accepted the cigar and watched him puff on the end of his. She copied his motions and puffed too.

"Let the smoke linger in your mouth, exhale. You're a natural."

"My mother would fall over dead if she saw me smoking a cigar." She blew a perfect circle and smiled. "College."

He grinned. "Tied to your mother's apron strings? At thirty?" He dipped his thumb into the brandy and wiped the pad over her lower lip.

Oh yes. Definitely out of her comfort zone. She touched her lip, then laughed and puffed again. "The strings were cut a long time ago, but she worries. I'm her only child."

"Your father?"

"They're divorced." Sarah didn't want to ruin the

moment by bringing up anything negative. "I understand how you feel about Bella."

Franco's eyes dimmed but then he turned toward the ocean view, hiding his pain from her. It made her feel as if she lost something.

She crossed her legs and sat back against the cushion. If they were to be friends, then she supposed quiet moments were allowed. It beat the hell out of worrying over whether or not he liked her the way she liked him. *And I do.*

He leaned forward, his elbows on his knees as he smoked, sipped and studied the horizon. "These are Catelli," he said, lifting the cigar. "Smooth."

"As my first, and probably only, cigar, it's been great." Sarah liked holding it in her fingers, alternating puffs and drinks. Tiny drinks. "This is a whole new level for me. I'm usually a beer on the pier kind of girl."

Franco turned toward her with enthusiasm. "You paddle board? It's the perfect ocean to do it. I'm teaching Bella." He puffed, looking suave. "Maybe you could help?"

"Of course!" As a friend, she told herself.

"Do you fish? Tell me about Sarah, away from the shelter. You seem more relaxed tonight."

"Dinner was amazing." *And the company.* She swirled the inch of brandy left in her glass. "I am just Sarah. No matter where I am. If there's a sea turtle that needs rescuing, I'm in. Manatees, sea rays, you name it.

On land, I'm all about protecting unwanted pets from being tossed away like trash. It breaks my heart, seeing how easily an animal can be discarded."

"You are passionate," Franco said, his eyes darkening. Calling to her.

Was she?

"I suppose I am. Yes." She laughed to sever the desire between them. "But I won't bore you with my soap box. I can talk spay and neutering all night."

Franco blinked, releasing her from temptation as she'd hoped. His intensity challenged her. Made her think of sensual things instead of what was practical.

"What else?" he asked, nudging her bare knee with his brandy glass. "More?" He added some of the amber liquid to his, but Sarah declined.

"I really am on call. If I go away somewhere, Martin covers for me, but that's only happened twice in the last year."

"You are very dedicated."

"Which doesn't leave much room for a social life, I know. Yes, I fish. I have a few friends that hang out at the pier, too. If you'd like, I can ask if Danny would show you his kite sail?"

"No, no. But if the weather is nice, I want to take Bella snorkeling this weekend. Would you like to join us?"

Sarah kept her smile neutral, resisting the urge to press her mouth against Franco's and taste the brandy from his lips. "I'm working," she said with a shrug.

"Always working." Franco's gaze dropped to her chest, then down her dress to her feet. "Not always. You have a nice tan."

"Paddle boarding," she said, self-consciously. "Maybe I can get away for an hour or so. Where are you thinking to go?"

"Just out there," he said, pointing to the endless blue water. "There's plenty of room."

Sarah laughed. "There's a shipwreck snorkel trail, actually. Is Bella a strong swimmer?"

"Sure, but I have a small rubber boat for when we go out, too."

"Perfect." She set her empty glass on the wicker table. "If you go to the town website, they have the trail marked out. It's fun."

"I'd rather have you join us. A guide."

Sarah shifted on the couch, sitting up straight and folding her hands over her knee. Easy. Friendly. "Like I said, I'll try to get some free time."

Franco finished his cigar and brandy, lingering on the couch as the sun went down. Just past dusk, he stood and held out his hand for Sarah's. She placed her fingers over his and he tugged her upward. It would have been a simple move to bring her into his arms, to kiss her pink lips, press her soft breasts against his chest.

But no.

He did not have the right to act on his desires. Not with Sarah, of all people. She seemed a shining beacon of what was right in the world. There were days he wondered if he dragged darkness in his wake.

No more. He and Bella were on the mend, choosing to live in the light. But that didn't mean he was ready for a relationship. He was still figuring out how to be a dad.

"Can I interest you in an oatmeal cookie before you go?" Send her home with a glass of milk and get his priorities straight.

She pulled back, the flare of interest in her green eyes banked. "I would love one. Sure I can't help with dishes?"

"No! You are our guest." He put his hand on the small of her back as he gently pushed her toward the door leading into the dining room. She tensed. Was she affected as he was? *God.*

"Friends..." she said rather insistently.

"I won't hear of it." He had to get her out of the condo. Back into her khakis, though he would look at her differently in them now. "Bella! Come, show off your cookies for Sarah." He passed her, careful to keep himself to himself, and took the container down from the shelf.

"Can we have milk?" Bella shouted, racing into the kitchen.

He quickly cleared away the olives and cheese, taking down three short glasses and three saucers. He warmed the cookies in the microwave. *What would it be like to have Sarah around more often?*

"Those smell terrific," Sarah said, determined, it seemed, to keep pretending they didn't feel anything despite the pulsating awareness between them.

No pretending for him. Dishing out warmed cookies, he poured the milk and leaned back against the oven as the ladies sat at the bar. How could he be attracted to the woman who had made his life hell for the last two months?

"These are way better than my pumpkin dog treats," Sarah said after she finished her cookie.

"I don't know. If you package them properly, I could sell them in the store." So maybe he was creating a reason to keep her in his life. He wasn't sure if it was the right thing to do or not, but he followed his instincts.

"You would do that?" She tilted her head as she looked at him.

His body tightened beneath her direct gaze. "Why not?"

"I just, well." She twisted her hair back over her shoulder. "Martin and I were just talking about offering them for sale on the website, once I get them where I like. I never meant to get into the treat business."

"It's another income stream. Makes sense, yes?"

"That's really nice of you."

Franco pushed off the stove and collected the saucers to put in the sink. "I can be nice."

Sarah gave a soft laugh. "I started our friendship off on the wrong foot. With the citation. I'm sorry about that."

"Yes," Franco agreed. Is that what she thought they could be? Friends? Who was she kidding? Just herself. He wanted her in a way that went beyond sharing cooking recipes. Wanted, but couldn't have. He wasn't ready yet to let another woman into his heart.

"Forgive me?" she asked.

"I understand why you were so vigilant. Water under the bridge."

"I want some water," Bella said, her mouth rimmed in chocolate.

Franco took her empty milk cup, rinsed it, and filled it before handing it back. "There you go, princess."

"Thank you, Daddy."

"Thank you both," Sarah said, rising to leave.

"Think about what I said." He paused, meeting her eye to eye. "About the dog treats. I'll be in touch for Saturday."

"I'll see," Sarah said. "No promises. It's a hazard of the job."

"What is Saturday?" Bella asked, looking from Franco to Sarah.

"If the weather is nice, I thought we would go snorkeling."

"Yeah! And Sarah can come?"

Franco saved Sarah from trying to come up with

another excuse.

"Isabella, relax and wait to see. Why don't you tell Sarah good-bye, and go brush your teeth? It is bed time already."

His daughter slid down from the stool with great reluctance, but gave Sarah a hug. "Goodnight, Sarah. I liked your treats."

"Sweet dreams, Bella." Sarah pressed a kiss to the top of his daughter's head. He tensed at the sweet gesture. Had Bianca ever done that? Bella had been Bianca's possession. Her pawn.

Sarah walked toward the front door and collected her purse on the way. "You are an amazing cook," she said.

"It's my passion," Franco said, following her to the door. *Like you.* He watched the way her hips filled out the back of the short dress. For reasons he didn't fully understand, Sarah woke his libido and dared him to think outside Mr. Mom.

The sound of the water in the bathroom and the dog barking let him know his daughter was busy brushing her teeth.

"Passion." Sarah repeated the word, her back to him.

"Like you," he said aloud this time, wanting her to see they might have more in common than she thought. "I tend to follow them." He opened the front door, allowing her to go into the foyer. Then, because he had to, because if he didn't he would regret it, he caught her arm and pulled her close. "There is nothing wrong with passion."

He pressed his mouth to hers and tasted the sweetest lips he'd ever kissed. "I like you, Sarah, but we won't be friends."

Chapter Eight

Sarah stumbled to her truck and climbed in, her short dress hiking to her upper thighs. Did she care? No.

He kissed me. Holy shit, he kissed me. He smelled like brandy and tasted like spice, his lips firm, his tongue teasing the edges of her mouth. She didn't remember kissing being so hot, or she might have missed it more.

She knew he'd be great. His strong hands cradling her hips, his upper body melded to hers, his upper thigh slightly pressing against the juncture of her legs.

Not just a kiss, but a steaming hot melding of mouths

that brought to mind images of them together. Preferably naked.

She couldn't go swimming with him in the ocean. For one thing, she wouldn't be able to keep her hands to herself. She'd want to plunge her fingers in his thick, dark hair. Caress his broad, bare shoulders. And whatever else she could reach.

Like you, Sarah, I follow my passion.

She never would have been [illegible] that!

Pulling into the street toward home, she almost missed the turn because she kept reliving the way his hands had felt on her body.

Martin was right—she'd forgotten what it was like to be a woman. Should she start screaming about unmet needs?

Laughing at herself and her ridiculous, over-reactive response to Franco's hotness, she parked the truck. Her cell phone rang and her first thought was wondering if it would be him.

I like you, Sarah, but we are not friends.

What the hell did that mean, anyway?

She shook her head to clear it and read the screen. When she was away from work, she forwarded the Pet Rescue phone to her cell phone. Ah, hell. Talk about a buzz-kill.

"Pet Rescue, how can I help you?" At nine thirty on a Wednesday night?

"There's something stuck in the garbage can on my back porch." The woman's high tones conveyed her fear.

Sarah looked down at her pretty borrowed dress. Time to get back to the real world. "And you don't know what it is?"

"It's probably my neighbor's cat."

"Have you tried taking the lid off of your garbage can?" Sometimes people didn't think of the simple things.

The female voice lowered. "What if it isn't a cat?"

Sarah exhaled. She'd run into that before and had her friend Rick on speed dial. "What is your address?"

The woman rattled off something just a few blocks away.

"Could you please hurry? I'm worried. I don't want it to suffocate or anything."

In a trash can? "I'll be right there." Sarah kept an emergency pair of coveralls in the back of her truck and an old pair of sneakers just in case.

"I live alone," the woman said. "It's dark. You probably think I'm a wuss."

"I don't, actually," Sarah said, responding to the emotion in the woman's voice. She repeated what her mother had told her earlier. "We need to stick together."

"Okay. Thanks. I'm the house at the end of the block."

Sarah found the one-story rancher overgrown with tropical palms. There were no outside lights, which created a shadowy and spooky atmosphere. Swallowing hard, Sarah got out of the truck, and opened the back. Bite sticks, gloves and a net. She shimmied into the coveralls and stuffed her feet into the sneakers, hoping she wasn't disturbing any spiders since she had no socks.

The woman called from her front porch, "Hello?"

"It's me, Sarah Murphy." Sarah shut the back of her truck. "I'm coming."

"Thank you." The woman, middle-aged with graying hair, shorts and an oversized t-shirt, joined her at the edge of her lawn. "The rattling is getting louder."

Rattling? "No problem. As you can see, I've come prepared." Sarah lifted her tools, the coveralls bagging around her body.

"The neighbor's cat had kittens once under the back porch, which is why I wonder if one got caught in my trash can. They were so mad at me when I called the pest control people, but how was I to know, right?"

Sarah nodded. "We'll know in just a minute what you've got back there."

She went with the woman around the house, carefully following in her footsteps since there was no light.

"Here we go." The woman climbed the steps of the screened back porch, opening a squeaky door that aggravated whatever was in the trash can.

Sarah tightened her grip on the bite stick, and grabbed her net in the opposite hand. "You can go inside if you'd like. I'll take it from here."

The woman folded her arms and shook her head. "I just want to know."

"All right. Stand back." Sarah took a deep breath and lifted the trash can lid with the bite stick. Hoping to see whiskers and pointy ears, she was disappointed when she heard the clackity-clack scratching of nails against plastic.

"That doesn't sound like a cat," the woman said, her voice up a few octaves.

"No, ma'am." Sarah wished she could just put the lid back on and call it a day, but she had to know what was in there. A bird? A possum?

"Could it be a raccoon? What if it has rabies? I have dogs, you know. You'll have to take it. You're a no-kill shelter. I read that on your website."

"For dogs and cats, pets. Raccoons are pests."

And she wasn't sure that's what they were dealing with. Sarah set the net down and forced herself to pick up the garbage can lid and peer inside.

Snapping jaws greeted her from a furious young alligator and she jumped back, accidentally bumping into the woman, who screamed.

"Gator," Sarah said, quickly tightening the lid down as her adrenalin pumped through her body like an electric jolt—reminiscent of the hot kiss from Franco earlier. It was her night for sensory overload. "You have to call a different number for that."

"Will they hurry? You can't just keep a gator out here!" The woman was a bundle of nerves, her hands shaking as much as her voice.

"Let me give you their number. Don't worry. I'll sit with you until they get here."

"Thank you. I have small dogs, you know."

Got it lady. Sarah pulled her cell phone from her large front pocket. "I have them in my contact list. I'll just do it." She pressed the number, which rang five times before someone answered.

"Rick's Rodent Removal."

"Hey Rick, it's Sarah. How do you feel about alligators?"

"Nice," he answered gruffly, as if he'd been sleeping. Pest duty was also an all-hours gig. "How big? Do I need the dart gun?"

"I don't know. Probably not. About four feet at the most, tip to tail? And furious at being trapped in a garbage can for hours."

"I'm on it." He coughed, then released a loud sigh. "I am up. I am on my way. Hey Sarah, you have no idea how cushy you got it, running that shelter. I spent the earlier part of today wrestling a python in Cypress Swamp."

Sarah, for all her love of animals, didn't really care for snakes. "And how'd that go?"

Rick chuckled. "I won. Duh."

"Glad for that." She rattled off the address. "We're in the back. You'll need a flashlight."

By the time Rick removed the gator from the

woman's property, and the woman gratefully paid the pest removal bill, Sarah trudged back to her truck. No money in her pocket, but sometimes that was just how things went.

Sarah's phone rang again as she pulled into her parking spot. She automatically answered as she juggled her purse for the house key, which she kept on a separate ring so that Martin could borrow the truck as needed.

"Pet Rescue, how can we help you?"

"Hi honey, it's your mother. How was your date?"

"Mom, it was not a date. Just a nice dinner between friends."

"Friends? Not a thank you from a client, like it started out?"

Her mother was a freaking hound dog on the scent of some juicy news.

"*Friends.* The dress was great, by the way. I wore the green one."

"Well, no wonder he wanted to be friends. That dress is magical. I'm surprised he didn't steal a kiss."

Sarah sucked in a breath.

"Sarah? Was there a kiss?"

"I gotta go! I'll call you tomorrow, okay?"

She hung up, wishing she could turn off her phone, but part of the contract with the city was that she was on call in case of a pet emergency. Thinking about the contract made her think about the roof, which made her stomach hurt.

How could she come up with enough money to keep her business? She'd saved, and then the air conditioner broke and had to be replaced. The patch for the roof hadn't been cheap to begin with. Sarah dug in her console for an antacid then got out of the truck.

Sarah walked inside her apartment and flipped on the lights. The dogs were curled up, side by side, on the couch, like the best of pals.

"Hey guys!"

They barked, jumped off the couch and raced her down the hall. She undressed quickly, hanging the green miracle on a hanger on the back of her door. Sarah chose boxer shorts and a tank top to sleep in, keeping her phone within hearing distance.

"Want to go out?"

Sarah had a private courtyard with a patio and fence that allowed the dogs to have space to run. It might not be a view of the ocean, but it was home and she liked it. The dogs finished their duties in record time and when she asked them if they wanted a treat, they both eagerly watched to see what kind.

The pumpkin got extra moves from both of them. She made a cup of tea and went back outside, thinking over the kiss and what she would do about it. "It was awesome, guys. Electric. Probably not a good idea to do it again, you know? I'm not saying I'm going to do anything. But man, his kiss made me realize what I've been missing."

Her puppies curled up together on the giant dog bed she kept on the patio. Benny and Pippa had found each other in a dog-eat-dog world.

Maybe there was hope for her.

Franco couldn't believe he'd kissed Sarah. And now he was left with a hard on that had no intention of leaving any time soon. She'd responded, hot and heavy. Her mouth had been made for him, her lower lip plump and perfect for nuzzling.

And her hips? Good God, there would be no sleep tonight.

He got out of bed and walked to the window overlooking the beach. Pitch dark but for the occasional peek of the moon behind a cloud. When was the last time he'd even wanted to touch a woman?

But it was Sarah—just Sarah that woke up his senses. He brought up the image of her sitting back against the sofa on his balcony outside, that shimmering green dress resting at her tanned thighs, the brandy in one hand, the cigar in another.

Blowing smoke rings, for God's sake, like she'd done it all her life. What else had she learned at college?

Her hair was soft as corn silk, the colors similar. Yellow strands to the purest white. She was meant to be in the sun. Would she join them Saturday?

Now that he'd tasted her sweetness, there was no way he couldn't go back for another sip.

What of Bella? Dating—if he decided to date— as a single parent complicated things. Perhaps he shouldn't have companionship for himself until Bella was older. He regretted the thought. The image of how naturally Sarah had kissed Bella tonight, helping her off the stool, stuck in his mind.

What if Bella needed a woman in her life, too?

The right woman.

Franco pounded his fist against his palm. "Enough. We will take things one day at a time, just like we've learned to do."

So saying, he picked up his iPad and searched the snorkel trail, making a mental note to have the little boat serviced before Saturday.

He heard a sniffling sound and got up, his heart racing as he went down the hall toward his daughter's bedroom.

She slept with the door cracked open, as he did.

Paisley looked up from where she was curled in a ball at Bella's back. Her silky ears shot up, then she tucked herself back to sleep once she recognized Franco.

Bella flung her arm out. "Mama," she said, her voice breaking.

Mama?

"Wake up, Mama. Please wake up."

Franco's body broke out in chills. He'd made sure

Bella had therapy too, but she never talked about finding her mother, dead in the bathtub. The professionals said to give her time. That she was so young, she might repress the memory in order to heal.

He crossed the room in silent steps, pressing his hand gently to Bella's forehead as he sang her a song. A Brazilian lullaby meant to chase bad thoughts away.

You don't belong here, Bianca. Get out.

Franco would stand guard and make sure of it.

Chapter Nine

Franco flipped a blueberry pancake and checked the clock on the microwave above the stove. Fifteen minutes extra sleep for Bella, since she hadn't slept well. Damn Bianca anyway. He set the pan to the back burner and walked into Bella's room and switched on the light.

"Morning, princess. Time to get up before I give Paisley all of your blueberry pancakes." The puppy yipped excitedly.

Bella sat up in bed, her hair a cloud of chaos around her small face. Olive-skinned with oval, dark eyes his daughter tugged at his heart. Bianca had been blue-eyed with paler skin and chestnut hair perfected in a salon, a petite woman who photographed even better than she looked. It was too bad that people's insides and outsides didn't match, like he and Bella had talked about.

It would sure make things easier.

"Daddy, doooon't!"

"I was just teasing, Isabella. No tears."

It was too late. He should have known better, after a rough night, to think she might be in the mood for jokes. Franco pulled her from bed, flinging her over his shoulder as she cried.

"You get special treatment today! Carried to the breakfast table so that your princess feet do not even have to touch the ground!"

"Daddy," Bella giggled through her sobs. "Put me down. I can walk."

"All right." He set her down, realizing that her blue pajamas, covered with trains and elephants, were getting short at the ankle. "Bella, I think you are getting taller."

"I am?" She climbed into her chair at the small round breakfast table. "I want to be as tall as, as," she frowned, thinking of something. "As you, Daddy."

"I would like that, but you need to eat your pancakes."

She cut into the one he had waiting. "I want to be tall," Bella said. "Not round."

Franco laughed. "People come in all shapes and

sizes."

"Not square. Or triangle."

"True. Maybe you do not need to go to school today, since you are so smart, Miss Isabella de Silva."

"I do need to go!" She finished her pancake and drank her milk. "I like school."

"I am glad that you do." Franco topped off his coffee from the pot he had brewing on the counter. "What are you doing today?"

"We have a math test. I'm going to get an A. What are you going to do today?"

"I am going to order supplies. And check a breeder who wants to sell a Chihuahua-Poodle mix. A chi-poo."

Bella started to laugh. "You said poo."

"I know," Franco said, shaking his head as he drank the dark roast he preferred. "I think they'll sell."

"Like Sarah's dog treats?"

"We will see," Franco said, hiding his immediate reaction to hearing Sarah's name. He'd finally succeeded in putting her to the back of his mind, and now here she was, front and center. "If she wants to put the effort into getting something together, we can help her."

"That would be nice, Daddy." Bella got up from her chair, bringing her plate and empty glass to the sink. "Thank you for pancakes. Blueberry are my favorite."

"You think I don't know that?" Franco finished his mug and set it on the counter. "Race you. Twenty minutes before we get to the front door. Go!"

He'd already taken care of Paisley and all he had left to do was grab his iPad, phone and put the dishes in the dishwasher. Since Franco had fired the last nanny, he hadn't bothered with getting another one. He'd already been doing the household duties.

Funny, how "chores" provided boundaries.

He used to hate them as a kid, but did them anyway or his allowance was zero.

As an adult, it was a privilege to have a full time staff. Not one he wanted at this stage in Bella's life. Maybe once she was older…right now, being immersed in routine and family was what she needed, and Franco was determined to give it to her.

"I win," she said, standing by the door wearing her school uniform, her backpack at her feet.

"It was close," he said, grabbing the keys to his Volvo.

"Close doesn't count," she said, darting toward the elevator to press the button.

"Where did you hear that?"

"From you!" Bella laughed and got in, pushing the L for Lobby.

They waved to Bob, then went to the carport. They'd only been doing this for two months, but they were getting it down to seven minutes flat. He dropped her off at a private charter school that had plenty of educated staff and no budget cut worries.

The silver-haired principal was there to greet the

parents in car line, and she waved to him as he pulled to the curb.

His daughter got out under the watchful eye of three teachers. "Bye Daddy!"

"Good luck on your test, Bella," he said.

The drive from school to the pet store was nine minutes, or thirteen if he caught the drawbridge.

Today it was nine, giving him plenty of time to open the store and get online to order supplies before things got crazy.

He entered in through the back, and Myra was already there, cleaning the animal pens. "Morning," he said. Franco had five employees, all dedicated to the well-being of the puppies. They'd been just as furious about the citation as he had been, and now kept a look out for Sarah, or her employee, Martin.

"I really thought I might beat you here," he told her. She was about forty years old, with a pretty face and a friendly smile. Myra wore her thirty extra pounds with grace, and had a laugh that welcomed everybody who walked in the front door. Her hair ranged from blonde to red to brown, depending on the color that spoke to her that month.

"I wake up and can't help thinking of these little darlings alone in here. I bring my coffee with me," she said. "I don't mind."

"I appreciate it," Franco said, deciding that a raise might be in order at her six month review. "Did you check out the chi-poo?"

Myra rolled her eyes. "What will they think of next? Adorable, but wow…"

"I'm going to do some more research before I say yes, but the breeder looks legitimate and of course, Dr. Wilton will have to examine the puppies."

"You go that extra mile," Myra said, squeezing between the aisles with a sponge and rubber gloves. Since that first week in business, they'd switched to all natural cleaning products that seemed to be made mostly of vinegar and lavender.

"We get a lot of foot traffic, which is nice. But a lot of it is tourists. I wasn't sure that people traveling would buy puppies, yet it seems that they do." Not his idea of souvenir. Easier to pack a t-shirt or a sand dollar.

"Oh! We sold the last Maltese last night." Her voice thickened. "Such a cutie pie, but the couple fell in love, you could just see it."

"Good." Franco really liked making people happy. "I brought in some new treats. What do you think of these?" He brought out the plastic container of pumpkin rye bones. "You can eat them."

"Seriously?" Myra asked, looking at him over the rim of her red rhinestone glasses.

"Yes." He grinned.

She took a very, very small bite, then nodded with surprise. "I like that hit of molasses in there. Where did you get them?"

"I know someone who makes them from scratch. All natural. Five ingredients."

"They'd sell here." Myra shrugged. "People like designer stuff, they like all natural. Why not? Let me know when you need the shelf space." She grabbed a roll of paper towels. "People are strange. Telling them they could eat their dog's treats? We should probably hike up the price. I like it, Boss."

Would Myra be so happy when she found out that Sarah from Animal Control was the baker? Franco decided not to borrow trouble.

Sarah walked into Pet Rescue at ten minutes after eight in the morning. She wore long khakis and a white polo, her hair back in a bun, the quickest solution for the rat's nest. She was rarely late, but last night's extracurricular alligator capture left her exhausted. She refused to consider that it might have anything to do with her dreams of Franco.

Benny and Pippa raced inside, going straight for Nashville's bed by the window. They felt that it was their job to make sure she was awake as soon as they arrived.

The cranky old cat hissed at them and, securely out of their doggy reach, swatted her tail and closed her eye.

"Morning to you, too, Nashville," Sarah said with a laugh. Despite her lack of sleep and her tardiness, she was in a fine mood. She didn't pick apart the reason why.

By the time Martin strolled in at ten, she'd already walked all the dogs and cleaned out the pens and had started a new batch of treats.

"Whatever you're making," Martin called as he came in from the warehouse, "I'll have two. It smells like dessert." He patted his nonexistent hips. "I can take it."

Sarah grinned, wiped down the counter and set the timer for half an hour. "These are berry. So far so good." She pointed to Benny and Pippa, who both slept on their backs, their little tummies full. "Even Nashville likes them."

"You might have something, here," Martin said, taking a nip of a paw-shaped treat.

"If you want to help me brainstorm, Franco said that he would sell these in his shop. He has customers willing to pay top dollar."

"Franco? Not Mr. de Silva?" Martin slid around the table to peer into her eyes. "What happened since yesterday after I left?"

Sarah gave him the quick run-down. "So, I went there for dinner. And I even wore a dress."

Martin pretended to have a heart attack and sank back into the chair at the table. "I've seen you with your hair down. I'm sure he was pleasantly surprised."

To tell him about the kiss? To keep it to herself? Her smile widened. "He makes excellent steak, and it was his idea to add the honey to the pumpkin, and cut the rye with wheat flour so the treats wouldn't be so heavy."

"I take it he's off the watch list now?"

Sarah opened the refrigerator and pulled out the carrot juice. "We need to stay aware, but I don't think he's that kind of guy."

"So he's gorgeous, he can cook, and he's a gazillionaire. What kind of guy is he? Oh yes, I know. *Single.*" Martin nodded as she lifted the jug of juice in his direction. "Perfect for you, Sarah."

She took down two glasses and poured carrot juice into them. She handed one to Martin, and kept the other in her hand. "He's a dad. Don't forget that part." She'd been reminding herself of that all night. "You don't have fly-by-night relationships with people who have kids."

Martin drank slowly. "Mmm. I love this stuff. And why not? Everybody needs a little special attention. Even daddies."

"It wouldn't be fair to Bella." *Or me.* "I don't have time, anyway, not to mention that dinner last night was a simple thank you. Nothing more, nothing less." She'd finally fallen asleep to that mantra running through her head. *Just a kiss. Just a kiss. Just a kiss.*

"You know best, Sarah." He reached for a pen in his pocket. "So what can I help you brainstorm about?"

"Packaging." She crossed her arms and gnawed her lower lip. "How can we make these look cute?"

"I *like* the paw prints and the bone shapes."

"Outside packaging," Sarah clarified. "Pink

cellophane, maybe?"

"Oh. Hmm." He frowned, tapping the table with the pen. "That sounds…cheap."

Sarah winced. "Yeah. Even with curly ribbon tied around the top?"

"I don't want to crush your dreams, Sarah, but if you want to sell at a high-end designer dog store, you need to think outside the plastic bag."

"So what do you got, Martin?" She'd maxed out loans to get this property. Reached the limits on her two credit cards to keep food on the shelves. "I have to get this roof done and it looks like these treats might be another income stream." *Thank you, Franco.*

"I am all about champagne dreams on a beer budget," he said, batting his lashes. "And there is more to it than glitter and flash. I make my own costumes and I learned a long time ago that appearance is everything. From a distance. Satin is affordable, while silk is not. From far away, sateen is even better."

"Sateen?"

"Falls apart in the wash, but for the few wears? Dynamite!"

Sarah picked up Pippa and laughed. "Maybe not *that* cheap."

He took the pad kept by the phone for messages that she'd had on the kitchen table and bounced the end of his pen to his lower lip. "Let's get down to business. How much for the ingredients? We need to price out how much each individual treat costs. Then you decide what the profit should be. There is room for a large mark-up."

"I don't want to rob people!" Sarah said, eyeing the figures. "But I do want to pay for that roof. Without doing a car wash. Which reminds me, I still haven't heard back from Courtney."

"About another extension?" Martin looked up and blinked, his brown eyes lightly lined in a darker brown.

"I'm hoping that once she hears my plan for making money, she might give me another few months." Sarah looked at the figures on the pad. "We need that roof. The box of 24 treats should sell for ten dollars."

"Now you're thinking like a business woman," Martin said with approval. "If we can sell what, a thousand, in the next month? Will that be enough?"

She pulled the pad toward her and did a few more calculations. "1300 boxes. If we can sell that many? I will have the money for the roof." For the first time in months she felt a glimmer of hope.

"Does that include the containers?"

She shook her head and held on as the emotional roller coaster dipped again.

"1500. I know a place that sells clear glass jars in bulk. Nice ones that look like crystal. I'll make a phone call. We can try," Martin said, standing up.

1500? That sounded completely crazy. She was the Girl Scout that never sold enough boxes to win a prize. "Thank you, Martin." The timer beeped and she hopped to her feet, quickly taking the tray from the oven and setting it on the stove.

"You did it, Chiquita," he said as he eyed the treats proudly. "Those look good. Um. I don't want to stress you out, about the money? But if you want to take your treats to the next level and sell them, we need to send them in for analysis. I've got the information up on our computer." He pointed toward the desk.

Analysis? That didn't sound affordable. Or quick. Sarah bowed her head.

The front door buzzer chimed, and they walked out of the kitchen. Her mom waved her hands and said, "Tell me about the kiss!"

Martin looked at her with disbelief. "Kiss?"

Sarah wished she could disappear through the air vents, but no.

"Jennifer," Martin said, walking toward her mother with his hands outstretched. "What are you talking about? Sarah didn't mention a kiss."

"Well, that makes me feel better. My blood was hot, thinking you two were here talking about Sarah's romantic evening without me."

"I didn't mention it because I didn't want to go there. We are not gossiping about my love life." Sarah blushed. "Or my lack of a love life. Okay? If you want to stick around, Mom, we are discussing designer dog treats."

Her mom wore bronze glasses today instead of her blue pair, with her hair down in a bob at her shoulders.

She paired her brown dress with copper and bronze jewelry with awesome leather heels. Adjusting her wallet purse, her mom stomped toward the kitchen. "Fine. I'm in. Any coffee left?"

"Mom..."

Sarah followed her mom, who stopped at the tray of treats then turned toward Pippa and Benny. "Yum! I see those two are happy little dogs," she said. "Their bellies look ready to explode."

"Happy dogs," Sarah said, shivers traipsing up her neck. "Does that ring any marketing bells?"

"I like it." Martin pulled at his waist band, centering the buckle of his belt. "Simple. But it doesn't convey the entire message."

"Happy Dog Treats?" her mom suggested.

"Hmm," Sarah said, her mind mulling over different names. "What about Happy Treat Bakery?"

Martin and her mother both clapped their approval. "You can have an entire Happy line of treats. Cats, rabbits, iguanas," her mom said.

Laughing, Sarah wrote the words out on the pad of paper. "This might be the next evolution of Sarah Murphy, business owner." What was one more hat?

"Will that affect the non-profit status of Pet Rescue?" her mom asked. "I know that your job for the city is by contract, so it should be something you can separate, too."

Sarah paced around the small kitchen. "I'll call my

accountant, just to ask what the logistics are. Mom, I have a bunch of things you can help me with, starting with making the dog treats legal." She jotted a note down on a post-it and stuck it against the refrigerator. "What's important is that if we sell treats, I can get the roof fixed. Maybe give Martin a raise."

"Did you say get the roof fixed, honey? Oh, thank heavens." Her mom covered her heart with both hands.

"Don't worry about the raise," Martin said.

Sarah hugged her mom. "You worry. I told Franco last night that worrying is what a parent does. Not that I know, but I've survived you doing it to me."

"Franco, huh?" Her mom linked arms with Martin as if they were a team, and Sarah had better hop to it. "Let's talk about exactly what happened last night at this dinner that you say wasn't a date."

Chapter Ten

Saturday morning, Sarah was inundated with rescue calls. A kitten in a pond, a barking dog that lived at a home she'd cited before for leaving the dog alone. She fined them and wrote on the ticket that if it happened again, they would go to court.

She hated the idea of the dog being so miserable that it just barked all day, so she included literature with the ticket on how to keep the dog occupied and happy while the owner was away. She understood that people had to work, but owning a pet was a responsibility.

As she drove away from the house, her cell phone rang again. "Pet Rescue, how can we help you today?"

"Hi, Sarah, it's Franco de Silva."

Her heart stopped, then started again with a thud. She'd put him from her mind, having heard nothing from him since dinner. Their kiss. Instead, she'd poured her energy into perfecting the baked dog treats.

Even if she never heard from Franco again, she could sell the treats on her own website and at the Farmer's Market. Her idea for a formal, high-end fundraiser was on hold until Courtney, who was the coordinator for the city as well as her friend, returned on Monday.

"Sarah? Are you there?"

Silence. Another great impression. "Hi!" Her voice hitched. "How are you?" Her palms grew damp and her pulse triple-timed it.

"Wonderful. Bella and I were hoping that you'd have time to meet us today, to go snorkeling."

She pulled over under a shady laurel oak so she didn't wreck her truck while acting like such a freaking girl. How could one person affect your breathing, for heaven's sake?

"We've been really busy all morning. I don't know that I can commit to anything. Some days are like that." She stared out at the empty sidewalk.

"What does a busy morning consist of?" he asked.

"Cats in trees, dogs in the neighbor's trash, returning escaped dogs, mostly." *How boring.* "Last week I had an alligator call." She thunked her head against the steering wheel.

"Exciting!"

"Well..." She rolled her eyes, glad nobody could see her silly reaction to his call.

"How are the treats coming?"

"The Berrylicious Biscuits are a real hit," she laughed. "Pippa isn't a big fruit fan, but even she likes them. I can send some over for Paisley, if you'd like."

"That would be nice."

Awkward, on her end, silence hung in the air. Why didn't she ever know what to say?

"Well." Franco cleared his throat. "If you get the chance, we will be by the pier around three this afternoon. Uh, do you know anything about birthday parties?"

"I've had a few." Where was he going with this?

"Bella was invited to a party for one of the girls from her class. I was hoping you could help me and Bella pick out a gift. I have no idea what would be appropriate."

"Uh." She shook the phone and smacked her forehead. Friends. Friends. Friends. "Of course I can."

"So, let's touch base later today? Do you have snorkeling equipment? I really hope you can make it."

"I'll do my best." Martin had already agreed to cover the phones for a few hours this afternoon, since he couldn't do the Farmer's Market tomorrow. "I have stuff in my truck. If you need anything, the Dive Shop carries kid's sizes too. Thanks for calling, Franco."

"*Tchau*, Sarah."

Even the way he got off the phone was charming, while she was a dud. Did she really have to bring up the alligator? He was probably laughing at her swamp-girl awkwardness.

But he'd called. *He didn't have to call.*

She started the truck and headed back to the office. Sarah made a deal with herself that if there were no calls for an hour, she would go snorkeling.

But if it stayed busy?

She couldn't do that to Martin. It wasn't fair.

By one o'clock, the phone calls had stopped, so Sarah went back to the warehouse where Martin was playing with the dogs in between grooming them for the Farmer's Market tomorrow. That was where most of her pets found forever homes.

"Hi, Martin. I've decided to take off for a few hours. Are you still okay here?"

"Sure! What's up?"

"I'm going to get in some beach time."

"Good idea. Enjoy." He shivered.

"I don't know why you don't like the water."

"I love the water. I don't like the sharks that would eat me in one bite the minute I fell off the paddle board."

"I've offered to teach you! I'll keep the sharks away."

"No thank you, Sarah. Go—have fun. Are you meeting that wonderful kite sailor?"

"Huh-uh. Franco and Bella are snorkeling. I might join them for a while."

"Be careful."

"I told you, I'm not afraid of sharks."

"I meant of your heart, Sarah."

"My heart is not involved."

"I take that back, anyway. I say, risk it all. Everybody deserves a few wild loves that go wrong."

"First of all, I am not looking for love. Second of all, why would it go wrong?"

"I am speaking from experience. My own sad, sorry, experience. Never mind me." Martin patted the black and gray terrier mix at his feet. "Love is a beautiful thing."

"This isn't love, it's snorkeling. Listen, on my way back I thought I'd stop at Ambrosia to get some salad for a late lunch. Interested?"

"Delicious. Anything with pecans. And goat cheese. I adore goat cheese."

"I adore you, Martin. Thanks for covering. I'll be back by four."

Once her mind was made up, Sarah quickly changed into one of the many swimsuits she kept in the truck. Hot pink and orange, this one fit for paddle boarding and covered her rear end the best. She braided her hair, tossed on a cream-colored swimsuit cover up and grabbed a towel.

Sarah loved the water, loved the smell of the salt in the air, loved the feel of the breeze against her skin and sand under her toes.

"Ready or not," she muttered beneath her breath. Was she making a mistake? "Here I come."

Franco wasn't sure whether or not Sarah would actually show up, so he was happily surprised when she walked toward the rubber boat he and Bella had banked on the sand.

Along with a giant beach blanket, towels and a bag filled with water, apple slices, sunscreen and a first-aid kit. He'd filled the rubber boat and they'd used the water route from his condo to this spot on the beach. He and Bella had just had a snack and were drying off, getting ready to make a sand castle.

He had no expectations of Sarah, though his mood lightened as soon as he saw her.

"Sarah!" Bella ran for Sarah, her long dark braid smacking against her back and sand spewing behind her.

Sarah dropped her beach bag and caught Bella around the shoulders. "Hey there, pretty girl. Are you ready to hunt for treasure?"

"Daddy said we were going to look at shells and fishes."

"That sounds great too." Sarah looked up, her hands still on his daughter's shoulders, and Franco stepped back as if shoved. *Beautiful.*

"Hi, Sarah," he said, his voice low.

She was a goddess from the sea, her blonde hair in braids on either side of her face. A smattering of freckles across her nose, and a hint of a blush on her high cheekbones. Her eyes sparkled deep, mossy green and he knew he'd never seen a woman so naturally lovely.

"Mr. de Silva," she said, teasing.

He smiled. "Am I ever going to live that down?"

"Probably not."

"I had my reasons," he said.

"I know. Which is why we get to be friends." She dropped her bag on the corner of their blanket and kicked off her flip flops.

Friends? Was she really back at that old song again? They would be more than that if he had his way. The past few days had been difficult. He'd wanted to call her. Knew he shouldn't call her. He was healing, true. But what if he wasn't done yet? There was a lot at risk for him to pursue a relationship.

Just feeling desire was something to get used to.

"I want to swim!" Bella wore a fitted life jacket over her one piece bathing suit, and she tugged at the rope on the small rubber boat. She had a child-sized snorkel and mask and purple water shoes.

"You are too cute, Bella, you know that?" Sarah helped her bring the boat into the water, brushing by Franco as she lifted her cover up over her head and tossed it to the blanket. "You, too."

"Cute? Me?" He did his best not to look at Sarah in her bikini. But he couldn't be more aware of the way she smelled like sunscreen, coconut and pineapple, or the heat of her body—
Sarah—as she passed him by.

"Definitely. All right, if we take the boat out to the swim buoy, there?" Sarah, the ocean surf at her ankles, pointed out about fifteen feet. "We can see cannons and ballast. The city created an artificial reef for people to have fun with."

"What's ballast?" Bella asked, climbing into the boat with Sarah's help. Salt water dripped down the sides, drying in the sun. Three people could fit in it, though it would be tight, Franco surmised. He wouldn't mind squeezing in.

"That's what gets shot out of a cannon," Sarah said, briefly meeting his eyes. "Like on a pirate ship." She chose to stay in the water rather than get in the boat, but kept her hand on the rubber handle as if to guide it.

"I don't like pirates. My daddy will protect me."

Sarah's sweet smile made his belly knot. "I believe that's true. Until you learn to protect yourself." She pretended her snorkel was a sword as she lunged into the surf. "I'll teach you to fight off the pirates."

Bella looked uncertain. Franco put his hand on the other side of the rubber boat and directed it further into the water. The calm ocean had a few waves breaking close to shore, but his daughter was fearless, usually, unless there were pirates. He hadn't realized. "I will always protect you, Isabella. That's what daddy's do. They slay dragons too."

Sarah looked back over her shoulder, up to her waist in the aqua ocean. Lovely, she took his breath away. "Most dads have given up dragon slaying now that we're in the 21st century."

Franco stumbled, knocked back by a small wave. He'd been too busy looking at Sarah to see what was coming next. *Not good.*

They swam on each side of the boat, keeping Bella in the middle, until they reached the buoy. "Here we are," Sarah said, water drops shining like crystals from her light lashes. Her movements were graceful and languid as she swam around the front of the small boat. "Want to get out, Bella?"

Bella looked at Franco, who nodded. Bianca hadn't liked the water—because she didn't want to redo her make-up and hair. It was nice sharing something he enjoyed with a woman who liked it too. Sarah didn't care about superficial things. She was all about what mattered. *Heart.*

Bella stood up and Sarah and Franco held the boat as she squealed and jumped into the water. She giggled and splashed her way around, floating on her back and then swimming around the buoy. "Where's the cannon?"

"Down here," Sarah said, pointing below the surface.

Bella adjusted her goggles, then stuck her head in for a few seconds, coming up again for an exaggerated breath of air. "I see it!"

"Did you really?" Franco asked, putting his head under too. Sarah's nearly naked body kicked next to him. What would her skin feel like against his? Beneath the water, she pointed to an array of concrete cannon. Blue and yellow fish darted around the ballast. Sea sponges and conch thrived, and all so close to shore.

He lifted his head and wiped his face with his palm. "It really is something."

"Nothing like the Keys," Sarah said, using the back of her hand to clear her eyes. "But it's in our own backyard, which is good."

"Agreed."

They took turns diving down, showing Bella how to manage the snorkel. His daughter held her hand out to one of the blue fish, and it kissed her finger. Her smile of pure joy filled him and he knew he'd made the right decision to move them here for a new life.

Nothing shallow, just being in the moment with the people that counted. Sarah fit in with him and Bella as if she were a missing piece.

They played and swam until Sarah tapped her watch and they bobbed to the surface.

"I have to get back. I'm sorry, because this has been a fun afternoon. I love the ocean! And seeing it through Bella's eyes brings me back to when I would come with my cousins as a kid. Thank you."

Franco nodded, not wanting Sarah to go. But he couldn't keep her with them when she had things to do. When was the next time he would see her? *Get a hold of yourself, man.*

"We're just glad you could come, right Bella?"

His daughter grinned. "I like being a pirate and searching for treasure. I want to do it again."

"Sounds great to me," Sarah said.

"Ready to go, Bella?"

"I'm hungry, Daddy. I want to eat an elephant."

Franco laughed. "I think the saying is 'I am so hungry I could eat an elephant', but if you want to eat wrinkly, smelly elephant then I can call the butcher and see what he has."

Bella thought about that, then looked at Sarah. "Would you eat an elephant?"

Sarah held on to the edge of the boat and shook her head. "No, Bella, I would not eat an elephant. I'll try a lot of things, but not that."

"What have you tried?" Bella asked as Franco helped her up and over into the boat. His daughter was so tired she felt boneless.

"Alligator, frog legs. Snails." Sarah sent him an apologetic glance. "Deer. I didn't like that at all."

"Venison, cooked well, is delicious," Franco countered. He imagined cooking for her. Candlelight. Wine. By the time she tasted his venison with potatoes and leeks she would change her mind.

"This was jerky, and I wasn't a fan," she said.

He pulled the boat string as Sarah pushed and they swam toward shore.

"I would love to cook it for you." He would like to make her laugh. Or to see the look in her eyes after he'd kissed her. Did she remember that at all?

"You have serious kitchen skills," she said, meeting his gaze around the boat and blinking away the water. "I would try it."

"I don't want to eat a deer," Bella declared. "They are *cute.*"

"Cows are cute, and we eat those," Sarah teased.

"Cows smell."

"Where have you been taking her?" Sarah stopped swimming once they could touch bottom again. The pink and orange bikini top filled out nicely, the tips of her braids falling over her breasts. Franco put his feet down, and the water came to his waist. A good thing to have his lower body covered. Now that he was aware of her, he couldn't stop thinking of anything but the two of them. *Together.* He forced the image away.

"We went to pick up some puppies in Ocala, at a dairy farm," Franco said, surprised at how normal his voice sounded. "Bella wasn't impressed with the smell of manure."

Bella blew a sound like a trumpet. "Gas, Sarah. Daddy said the cows make gas. Pewee." Seeing that they were so close to shore, she jumped out of the boat again.

"Fair enough," Sarah said, watching Bella splash. "Where did she see a deer?" she asked Franco under her breath.

"The petting zoo?" Franco thought back. "She liked the little deer and the goats."

"Better not introduce her to baby chicks, or you'll have a vegetarian on your hands." Sarah rested her fingers on his forearm and the feel of her sent a jolt rushing through him. "And that might be challenging to your cheffing."

"Cheffing?"

"Well, you do more than cook. What would be the right verb for what you do? Culinary magic?"

Her touch lingered and Franco's arm tingled. "You flatter me."

"I want another invitation to dinner. My mother didn't raise a fool." She met his eyes. "Not when it comes to eating well, anyway. I seem to be very foolish in other areas of my life lately." She tapped her finger to her pink lower lip.

He knew what she was referring to, and it took all of his willpower to keep his hands to himself. But damn, he ached to hold her, grab her by the shoulders and sink them both beneath the waves. The woman could kiss.

"Daddy! Watch this!"

He turned and felt the loss of Sarah as she pulled away toward shore. "I'm sure I'll see you guys around," she called.

He waved at Bella then watched Sarah walk from the ocean. Strong legs, straight back, gorgeous hips. Amazing ass. Franco felt a physical ache as she left the water. He waited a while, letting Bella play until he'd calmed his hormones and Sarah was long gone.

"Come on, princess. Time to go. How about some dolphin fingers at Anglin's?"

She rubbed her belly. "With fries?"

"You got it."

"I wish Sarah could stay and play with me all day long."

He wished the same thing.

"Let's go. You will have to make do with spending your time with me. We can go see the puppies after we eat. And get a present for the birthday party." He'd forgotten to ask Sarah what she'd recommend for a gift. Oh well, Myra would know.

He pulled the small rubber boat to the shore. He knew the manager at the pier and he could store his boat and belongings there.

"Do you have to work, Daddy?"

"No." Owning a pet store was new to him. Having employees and store hours. Management responsibilities. He'd always worked for himself.

"I could play with Elvira."

"Remember, princess, we don't name the puppies. They are for other people to adopt."

"I know." His daughter dug her toes in the sand and crossed her arms, her tone serious. "Sometimes Myra lets me sweep or wash the glass. People put fingerprints everywhere."

"Do you like the pet store, Bella?" He'd given up everything to start over, but it didn't feel like a sacrifice. His daughter wanted a puppy, he bought her a store. A new beginning, if his daughter was happy. No memories of Bianca here, or drugs or neglect. He knew that Sarah would never treat her children like that. Why hadn't she married, already?

Bella took a towel from their beach bag and Franco helped wrap it around her like a dress. "Yes. But not as much as I like dolphin fingers."

Chapter Eleven

Sarah chose navy shorts and a beige polo with her ankle boots to wear to the Farmer's Market. They had a 10 by 10 tent, with two chairs and a long white plastic table. Her plan this Sunday was to find the kittens homes. They usually went pretty quick, because who didn't want to take care of something soft, furry and helpless? And really stinking cute.

This was the third time for two of the dogs, though. The first for the gray and black mutt. He looked more like a puppy, so chances were good that he'd get adopted. It was harder for the older animals. And if they had issues? Near impossible. Benny, Pippa and Nashville belonged to her, now. They were her family.

As she came inside the office from her last load of animals in the truck she said to her mother, "I really hope I'm not destined to become some spinster old lady with three-legged dogs and one-eyed cats."

Jennifer, dressed in jeans and a beige polo, snorted with surprise. "The choice is yours. Stop adopting the ones that walk into walls. Same advice goes for finding a boyfriend."

"Since when did you turn into Ask Abby?" Sarah lugged the folded crates out the front door of Pet Rescue to the truck. Only the kittens left to grab, and then they could head out. "I'm not looking for a boyfriend."

On her way back inside her mom said in a too-casual voice, "I was asked on a date yesterday."

Sarah stopped so fast she sprained something in her calf. "And?" She leaned against the shelves in the foyer and rubbed the twinge in her leg. A date? Her mom? She'd assumed her mom had brought up the boyfriend comment to try and get more information about Franco.

"I said no."

Disappointment washed over her. "Why?" Jennifer Murphy was beautiful, fun and she shouldn't be alone if she wanted to have company.

"I was married to your father for a very long time."

"And then he left you for a bimbo. We're over it,

right?" Sarah realized that her mom, single for years, wasn't even fifty-five.

"I don't know how to date."

"I didn't have a clue that you were interested," Sarah confessed, feeling like a jerk for not seeing it sooner. She smacked her calf muscle.

"I wasn't. But," she shrugged. "He's a guy from work."

"Cute?"

"He's a middle-aged man, not a puppy!" Her mom smiled. "But he's got all of this beautiful silver hair."

"I think you should go," Sarah said.

Her mom actually blushed. "I don't know what to do. And you're so focused on work that you never spent time dating either, so you're no help."

Sarah spread her arms out, unable to get mad since her mother had a point. "We can ask Martin tomorrow. He'll know what to do. Or you could ask your friends."

"It's too embarrassing." Her mom shook her head and walked toward the door and the waiting truck.

"I feel like I have no clue who you are right now. Hang on a sec." Sarah dipped into the connected warehouse. "We can talk about this over coffee while we find homes for these guys." She thought of her mom with someone on her arm. Someone to go to the movies with, or walk on the beach. She eyed the mewling pile of gray and white fur-babies. "Hey, does your boy toy want a kitten?"

"Sarah Jane!"

"What?"

They reached the Farmer's Market a half hour before it opened to the public, giving them time to set up the crates and the table.

"Did you get the brochures, Mom?"

"Yes. It looks like it's time to re-order, though." Jennifer held up the thin stack of glossy tri-folded papers.

"Good, I'll be able to update them with the dog treats for sale."

"We can overnight a sample of your treats to a facility that stamps out what they're made of, for a label. We'll have to expedite it if we want them done by next week."

Sarah cringed. "How much?"

"I can help you with it. An early birthday present?"

"I just had my birthday a few months ago." Sarah reached out for her mom's hand. "Am I in over my head?"

Her mom gave her a half-smile. "You know what you want. I think you can do it. We can fundraise even without the treats."

"I ordered the jars yesterday. They'll be here for next week's market, if we get the labels in time?" She looked at the dogs, all three with their tongues lolling out. They were happy. Healthy. The kittens, too. It cost though. Food. Supplies. If she didn't have her shelter, these guys would be sent to one that euthanized. *No.* "I have to make it work."

"You will, honey."

"The roof needs to be done by the end of next month." Sarah heard her tone and decided to just be quiet for a few minutes until she could regain her positive attitude. Some days it was harder than others.

They got the three dogs situated in individual crates and the kittens shared a large one kept on top of the table. They plugged in fans to keep the area somewhat cool, then sat back to enjoy coffee her mom had brought in a thermos.

"We need an event to really kick-start sales of the treats," her mom said, legs crossed as she held a cup of coffee. "How about a car wash?"

Sarah loved her mother. Though sometimes she made her feel a little crazy, her mom's unwavering support gave her the strength to do just about anything.

"I was thinking about a classier sort of fundraiser…" She sipped her coffee, black and strong, from a paper cup. "Save the roof car wash? Who would I invite?"

"The whole city could get behind you. Guys like girls in bikinis."

"Well, I have a call into Courtney, she runs everything. I was hoping she'd have a good idea for something else. Like a dinner. A car wash?" Sarah flicked her cup. Car washes were not her thing.

"Keep it simple. You could have it at Pet Rescue. The parking lot is big enough." Her mom sat back in the plastic chair and stretched her legs out. Her pink sneakers with blue and purple laces matched the pink glasses perched on her nose.

Why not? She picked the first lame excuse she came up with. "I'd hate to disrupt the animals."

"They'd be inside the warehouse. What better way to get community support than to show them what you do? Where you are? Even better, Sarah, why you do what you do. Having people see the animals is *good*."

"When you put it like that, it's pretty smart, actually," Sarah admitted. She thought about how to open up the back area. "Let people know they can buy their pet supplies from me, too."

"I wish I could do more, Sarah. Financially."

Her mom had already helped her through college so that Sarah didn't have any school loans. Having a kid shouldn't be a life-long expense. Or was it? Sarah had made a point of getting the business loan on her own. "Mom, you're pretty awesome. I think it's really great that other people see it too. Go to dinner with this guy, get dessert. Walk on the beach."

Her mom smiled in thought. "We'll see if he asks again."

"You're going to make him work for it?" Sarah laughed.

"I don't want to be easy!"

Sarah put her empty cup on the closest dog crate, thinking of Franco and his kisses. The way she felt around him. *Alive*. "It might be fun."

"We'll see."

The first browsers passed by, pausing to check out the kittens, and Sarah got to work matching pets with people.

Hours later, she was down to two kittens out of the six she'd brought and the gray and black mutt with the friendly eyes was gone too. A nice family with three little boys had picked him right away.

"Two old guys left," Sarah said, bending down to unlatch their crates so they could get out and stretch a bit. She walked them on their leashes around the grassy area to the side of her tent, then came back, keeping out the all brown one with the sweet disposition. The other dog sometimes got cranky, so she put him inside his crate beneath the table.

"Oh, honey, that looks just like our MoJo."

Sarah turned at the sound of a woman's sad voice. She and her husband, probably in their mid-forties, walked hand in hand to the tent opening, where the husband refused to go further. The woman kept on toward the part Pit Bull mix as if she recognized a kindred spirit in the dog.

She dropped to her knees and took the dog's head gently between her hands. "Richard, this dog has the same markings, too. I can't believe it. He's for adoption?" The woman looked at Sarah, begging her to say yes.

"Of course," Sarah said, swallowing over the lump of emotion in her throat. "You can take him right home.

Well, there's some paperwork you have to fill out."

Richard said in a voice heavy with uncertainty, "Now, Kathy, you know we said that we wouldn't go through that again."

"How can you deny this dog a home, Richard? Look?" She got up and tugged at her husband until he came inside. "They could have been from the same litter."

Sarah felt their pain, mixed with hope. "What happened to MoJo?" she asked.

Richard coughed into his fist, his eyes damp. "Hit by a car. Died in our arms. Come on, Kathy. We agreed. It was too hard to lose him."

Kathy shook her head. "You said last week you were missing a dog in our lives." The dog woofed softly as she stepped back, thrusting his head beneath her hand. She blinked quickly, then put her husband's hand on the dog's soft head. "He needs us. He needs a home, and we have one."

"This is not MoJo," Richard said, his voice softening as his fingers scratched the dog's ears. His brown tail thumped the pavement, his body wiggling with repressed excitement though he didn't move from his spot.

Sarah turned and wiped her eyes, noticing that her mom was studying the ground pretty intently.

"Of course not. But still. Please, Richard?"

The dog chuffed, inching closer to the silently debating couple.

After a few moments, Richard got to one knee so that

he could look the dog in the eye. "Want to come home with us?"

The dog wagged his tail so hard his entire body shook, tongue to the side.

"All right, boy," he said. Richard turned to Sarah and said gruffly, "We'll need a collar and a leash."

"No problem. He's been fixed, and has all of his shots. He's very healthy. About seven, I think. I found him abandoned in an overgrown lot by the grocery store."

Kathy clutched her husband's arm as she helped him to his feet. "Thank you, Richard. You won't be sorry. You can take this one running, too."

Within twenty minutes, the dog was led from the Farmer's Market with his forever family. Richard wore the biggest smile as he thanked her.

"Oh, Sarah, honey. How can you do this? I thought I was going to cry."

"That's what makes it all worthwhile. Finding homes for the unwanted." She patted the crate with the last older dog and looked at the sleeping kittens. "We have another hour, Mom. If these guys don't go this week, they'll go next week. I don't get that many hits from the website. But I have a few ideas I want to try."

"I have always admired your perseverance. You knew what you wanted from the time you were little."

"Is that right?" a male voice asked. "Why am I not surprised?"

Franco's husky tones washed over Sarah and made it

difficult to catch her breath. She looked at him, and at Bella, who held a piece of roasted corn in one hand and her dad's fingers in the other.

"Franco! Bella. What are you guys doing here?"

"We like to walk to the market on the Sundays I don't work. I didn't realize that this was your booth. I try to steer clear of puppies when I'm off. What do you have?" Franco walked inside the tent and looked at the kittens, and the lone dog. "This is all that's left?"

"Yes." Her mother's curiosity rubbed like sandpaper. "Mom, this is Franco de Silva, and his daughter, Bella. My mother, Jennifer Murphy."

Franco held out his hand for her mom's and when Jennifer gave it, he brought the knuckles to his lips. "*Bom dia*!"

Charming. "That only works so well because of your accent," Sarah said, determined to put him at arm's length. She didn't know what to do with the feelings he roused in her. He wasn't a guy she could grab a beer with on the beach. He didn't inspire casual anything—including sex.

"Good morning, then," he said, smiling at straight at Sarah. He wore pleated plaid shorts, a white t-shirt and black slides on his feet. He'd invaded her dreams the last few nights—she needed the days to be Franco-free so she could concentrate on her business. "Do you like my accent?"

The deep rumble of his voice was like an aphrodisiac.

"I can see why you wore the green dress," her mom

said in a theatrical whisper.

He smelled like expensive aftershave and sunshine, not that she was noticing. Sarah put one hand up to her mother and the other toward Franco. "I don't always understand what you say," she told him before telling her mother, "I don't know what *you* are talking about."

Chuckling, Franco peered down at the dog Sarah brought out of the crate. "Long in the tooth, this one?"

"Yes. But some people prefer a mature dog to a puppy. As you know, they're a lot of work. Where is Paisley?"

"The dog is the size of a hamster and doesn't do well walking." Franco shrugged and tugged at Bella's hair. "I usually end up carrying this one part way. I only have two arms."

"Understandable." She wished he didn't look so good, or sound so enticing. He tempted her. Made her think beyond the work day. "What are you guys doing later?" She imagined another swim in the ocean.

"I'm going to visit a new breeder on the list."

"You check them out yourself?" Sarah nodded. "That's good. Without telling them who you are?"

"What?" He patted his chest and held one hand out in a 'who, me?' gesture. "I'm just an interested customer."

"Smart," her mom interjected. "If they knew you owned a designer puppy store they might charge more and change the set-up. You know my Sarah closed down the breeder that used to operate out of your shop?"

"I did know that," Franco said. "It caused a bit of tension, but we're over that now."

"Yeah. The best of friends." Sarah rolled her eyes. "Where are they located?"

"Alligator Alley."

"A two and a half hour drive..."Sarah said, doing the math.

"Not the way I drive," he said with assurance.

Her mother laughed.

Bella smacked her lips, slick with butter. "Daddy drives like NASCAR."

"And you wear your seatbelt?" Sarah asked. She could just see him zooming down the highway and a giant alligator crossing the road or something.

Franco and her mother both looked at her.

"What?" Sarah asked. "It's a logical question."

"I'm a very good driver," Franco told her, his nose a smidgeon out of joint.

"I'll add it to the list of things you excel at," Sarah said, not backing down because he was offended. Dads shouldn't be racing their daughters around in sports cars unless there were seat belts involved. Maybe not even then.

Her mother took off her glasses and listed her head slightly to the right. "Such as?"

Embarrassed, Sarah clarified. "Cooking. He used to cook for famous people."

"Anybody I know?" her mom asked, switching her

attention to Franco.

"Mom! Listen, I'd like to get these last animals adopted today, so if you don't mind, Franco," she said, hinting for him to leave.

Instead, he guided his daughter toward the chair Sarah had vacated and spread his arms wide. "I would love to help," he said. "I can take the old man here for a walk, and see if we get any takers."

The dog barked and wagged his tail as Franco attached the leash. "Franco, you don't have to do this. He's an older dog, and it's all right if he goes back to the shelter with me."

"I can do it. Do you think I can't find someone to adopt him?"

The man looked so good he could sell ice cream to Eskimos but that wasn't the point. Or was her pride in the way of just saying thank you?

"It has to be the right match," she cautioned. She followed him out of the tent and watched as he was immediately surrounded by ladies who admired the man holding the dog. "I can't believe it!"

"My daddy can find the dog a place to live." Bella, adorable in a plaid sundress and flip flops, finished the roasted corn and slid off the chair to put the foil and cob in the trash can under the table that held the brochures and the last two kittens. "Where are the good treats?"

"They'll be here next week." Sarah pulled her gaze away from the women surrounding Franco and walked to where the kittens slept. They blinked sleepy eyes and meowed as she opened the door to the crate. "Do you want to hold one, Bella?"

"Can I, please?"

"Sit back down." Sarah gestured toward the chair.

Her mother got up, helping Bella sit all the way back before Sarah handed her a kitten. "Gently, now," her mom said.

"I will be very very careful." Bella held her hands, palms up, and cradled the sleepy baby. "She's sooo cute!"

Her mom smiled. "Not as cute as you are, Miss Bella de Silva. You are in over your head, Sarah."

"I want one," the little girl said.

Ignoring her mother's comment, Sarah talked to Bella instead. "Your daddy said no already, and that's okay. I need people to hold the animals at the shelter all the time. You can help when you want to, all right?"

Bella grinned at Sarah before returning her attention to the sleeping kitten. "You are so nice, Sarah."

Sarah laughed, holding the other kitten close and walking back to the tent opening. Franco was in serious conversation with an older man, who reached down to pat the dog's head. "You were right, Bella. I think your dad found our dog a home."

Was there anything he couldn't do?

She was beginning to wonder.

Chapter Twelve

Getting the paperwork and the check, Franco watched the old dog and the old man walk off together and felt a buzz of satisfaction. "I think they'll be happy together," he told Sarah.

She eyed him with barely concealed amusement. "I was admittedly worried when you were talking to the women. Nobody who spends that much time in a salon is going to want a dog that farts."

Bella giggled and Jennifer Murphy admonished her daughter. "Sarah, really." She looked to Franco as if to say, what can you do?

He liked Sarah's mother, and really enjoyed seeing Sarah on a different level. As a daughter, instead of the one in charge, saving everybody all the time.

"So, Jennifer, tell us something about Sarah as a child. You were saying when we first got here that she always knew what she wanted to do."

"It's true."

Sarah groaned and started stacking the brochures. "Mom, no boring stories, okay?"

Franco wouldn't be bored by anything concerning Sarah. He'd even willingly listen to dance recital music, or watch family home videos. He waited expectantly.

"Nothing that comes from the heart is boring!" Jennifer gathered things together as she talked, efficient like Sarah. "When Sarah was ten, she found a dog by the side of the road. A collie mix." She shrugged. "Anyway, Sarah brought this dog home, and begged us to let her make posters and maybe even keep her. It was obvious she'd just had puppies, and the poor thing was a mess. Matted hair."

"Mom." Sarah gave her mother a pointed look, gesturing to Bella.

Jennifer nodded and Franco assumed that in mother-daughter language they'd just communicated to keep things child appropriate.

"Sarah's dad didn't really like animals so much so we took her to the pound. Sarah walked up and down the strip of road until she found the owners of the collie. It seems the dog had broken out of her pen days before. By the time we went to the pound," Jennifer trailed off but didn't finish her sentence.

Franco got it. They were too late to save the collie.

"Sarah runs a rescue despite the costs of upkeep for the pets for that reason. In fact, sad story aside, she's planning a fundraiser."

Sarah dropped her head and muttered something under her breath and Franco fought to hide his smile. "When?" Franco asked.

"We aren't sure yet, but we can let you know if you'd like to help."

Franco prepared to offer his checkbook, but Jennifer had something else in mind.

"Since you're a cook and all, why don't you man the grill? Hot dogs, hamburgers. I'm sure you can handle it." Jennifer smiled expectantly.

"Mom," Sarah said. "Franco is a *chef*, not a line cook at a burger joint. Franco, I'm sorry. Mom gets these ideas that she needs to help me out, and that's all there is." Sarah folded the table and set it next to the crates. Everything compact and easy to fit in the back of her truck. He appreciated her self-sufficiency.

"I never suggested that," her mother said, looking from Sarah to him. "I'm sure you're a whiz. She needs a new roof for the warehouse."

"Mom—"

"I would be happy to do it," Franco said. "Anything to help. Sarah, you showed me the roof already, remember?" Franco liked the idea of being part of the community, which is something that Sarah had already created for herself.

"Yes, but you don't have to flip burgers."

"I want to. I want Bella to learn the value of volunteering for worthy causes growing up, like I did. When I was twelve, I spent a summer picking fruit, separating the bruised pieces for jams. My grandmother insisted that every migrant worker was fed for the noon day meal, and at the end of each day, they could take a bag of fruit for their families."

"That's lovely. Where did you grow up?" Jennifer asked.

Franco saw that behind her pink glasses, she had blue eyes instead of Sarah's green.

"My family owned property along the Amazon, but then I moved to Bahia where I had a home. After my wife died," he barely paused and saw that Bella hadn't even flinched, which was progress, "we came here. It is quieter, tamer than our ancient city but just as beautiful."

"I've never been out of the country," Jennifer said. "Well, the Bahamas don't count since they're right across the way." She made a vague hand motion toward the ocean.

"No urge to travel and see the world?" He'd wanted to see, taste and experience everything. Having Bella had changed his priorities.

"I never thought about it," Jennifer said. "But why not?"

"Mom, you are full of surprises today." Sarah lifted her keys and shook them. "We should probably get going. It feels very strange to have found all of the animal's homes. Bella did great with the last kitten. The family saw how happy Bella looked playing with it that they really wanted it for their own."

"Good for business," Jennifer said proudly. "Now to get those treats sold."

"What do you think of them?" Franco asked.

"My dogs love them." Jennifer hiked her large pink purse up her arm. "I was fond of the berry ones myself."

Franco laughed. "I'm excited to hear your ideas for marketing, Sarah. Have you come up with anything?"

"Well, Martin and I brainstormed—he knows somebody that can get us inexpensive glass jars in bulk. I'm keeping it super simple."

He shook his head and shrugged. "Simple can work, but in order to sell to high-end clients, it can't look cheap."

She flinched as if he'd said something wrong. "I know that, Franco."

He held up his hand. "I did not mean to insult you," he said.

Sarah stuck her hands in her front pockets, her eyes glittering with hurt pride. "Maybe you can't help it. My reality is way different than yours. I am not buying cut crystal containers, all right? I can afford *glass*."

"Nothing wrong with that," he agreed. "It will just have to look the part." He wished he hadn't said anything. What did she mean, that their reality was different? Money? He was trying to help her!

Sarah backed up a few steps. "We thought of a name already too. Happy Treats Bakery. We can have an entire line of Happy treats." Her stance, feet planted and chin lifted, let him know she'd stand up for what she believed in. "We're going all-in starting this new business. In fact, we're sending the samples out for inspection this week."

"Be careful," he warned. "That can cost a lot when you aren't expecting it." Starting another business when the other one wasn't going well might not be in her best interest.

Impossible how high her chin hiked. Her shoulders went back, too.

"I've had my own businesses," she said in clipped tones. "I know what to do."

He didn't understand why she seemed so angry. "I have someone in mind for marketing. I can make a phone call."

"I can do this myself, Franco." She pulled her hands from her pockets, one hand fisted around her keys.

"As a favor to me," he said, wondering if she was upset by the possible cost. It was true he had money, but he viewed it as a means to an end.

"No, thank you."

"Sarah?" Jennifer asked. "Maybe a phone call isn't a bad idea. Getting a new business off the ground takes hard work, which you've done, honey. And a little bit of luck can't hurt."

Sarah's nostrils flared and she slipped her sunglasses on to cover her eyes but Franco could tell she was mad.

What in the hell was her problem? Her mom seemed willing to listen to reason. Hard work mattered, but an element of you who knew in the world mattered too.

"We can talk about this later," Franco said. "It's been a busy morning. And Bella and I still have to see the puppies."

Sarah's chin lowered and she turned her attention from her mother to him. "Really? What kind?"

"Chi-poo."

Bella burst out laughing and he put his hand on the top of her head as a reminder to keep their poo joke to themselves.

Sarah's lips twitched as she looked at Bella. He liked that she didn't take her anger out on anybody else. She didn't hold a grudge. "Oh?"

"What will they think of next?" Jennifer asked with surprise. "I can't imagine they'd be very cute!"

Bella piped up. "They are so ugly they are cute, Myra said."

"Who is Myra?" Sarah asked, and Franco wondered at the overly-casual inflection in her voice. Was she the smallest bit jealous? Or was that him, wishful thinking?

"She works at the pet store." Bella tilted her head. "She's nice."

"You should come in and meet her." Franco lifted his iPad, but that wasn't what was ringing. Myra might not take kindly to Sarah, now that he thought about it. As far as he was concerned, they were over the citation. Myra? Not so much. "See the chi-poo puppy, if we get one."

"Daddy, that's your phone," Bella laughed. She dug in his front jean's pocket and pulled it out. "Here."

He saw the number, but didn't recognize it. A text immediately followed.

"Well, Bella, it looks like we have our afternoon free." He swallowed disappointment, but then eyed Sarah. "They are rescheduling our meeting for tomorrow morning at ten."

Bella's lower lip stuck out and quivered. "I wanted to see a chi-poo."

"Did you say poo?" Franco asked.

Sarah looked at her mother, laughing at poo jokes as if she thought they were funny. Sarah would have been popped upside the head. Or maybe she was remembering a woman who had evolved since then, too. Change. Growth. *Grr.*

"So, can you help me, Sarah?"

Sarah pulled her attention to Franco, trying to let go of her anger. He had tons of money, so he probably didn't even realize that it was a touchy subject. But advising her to be careful as if she didn't know what she was doing? She shook her head. "I'm sorry? What did you say?"

"Come with me to check out the puppies tomorrow. The breeder says she's got eight for sale. That seems like a lot."

Her protective instincts rose to the fore. Eight would be a very large litter. "Unless she's combined two litters?"

"I can pick you up at seven," he offered.

Her mom looked at her with a twinkle behind her glasses. "I have tomorrow off from work, Sarah, so I can cover the phone for you. Leave the truck, and Martin will handle the calls."

If she said no now she'd look like a jerk, and she'd already way over-reacted to his offer of help. But dang it, he'd nicked her pride with his reaction to her glass jars, which were what she could afford. She didn't need a phone call to a marketing guy when she wasn't even sure she could sell a thousand boxes. What if the treats flopped?

Having her mom push her into Franco's car added to her irritability. Sarah was attracted to the man, plain and simple, but he was out of her league. According to him, she couldn't even be trusted with good taste.

Keep that separate, she told herself firmly. Busting bad breeders was her mission, and this was a great opportunity to check out one she'd never heard of before.

"All right," she said with less grace than she should have.

"Sarah, will you get the black one?" Bella asked as they all walked out of the tent. Somehow, Franco was carrying the crates and the table while she had the large box she'd kept the kittens in, and her mom had the plastic bins.

"We can see what they have, Bella. If they are healthy and your dad thinks that is the best one for your store, then we'll try."

Franco chuckled at her side. "That was a great non-answer. Satisfying without promising anything. I need to learn how to do that."

"You're doing fine." They reached her truck and together piled everything in the back. She softened, acknowledging his help with the oldest dog and the crates. And the treats, and the offer of a marketing guy. It was a lot for a woman used to scraping things together on her own. "You're a great dad."

Franco took Bella's hand. "I will see you in the morning, Sarah. It was a pleasure to meet you, Jennifer."

She and her mom waved and got into the cab of her truck.

"He is delicious, Sarah. You are in deep water. You don't have to save him, or his daughter. They are doing all right." Her mom sat back, checking him out in the side mirror.

"Agreed, he doesn't need saving. You're the one that just pushed us together for tomorrow!" And now she was nervous and knew she wouldn't sleep tonight. Again. "I don't need rescuing, either. Did you hear what he said?"

"Yeah. The big jerk offered to help," her mom said with an exaggerated laugh. "You don't have to do everything on your own."

Sarah clenched her jaw. She'd always done things that way. "Relying on other people is a recipe for disaster."

"Oh, Sarah. Bend a little. Flirt a little. Just be careful."

"How about you go out on your date, and leave me to helping a friend check out a new breeder. It's what I do, Mom. There is nothing between me and Franco."

Her mom took her glasses off and stared at her, hard. "Who are you kidding? He's attracted to you, Sarah. And you feel it too. How could you not? He's a sexy man. He's been wounded in life and that gives him an edge, and you, with your generous heart, can't help but want to mend him. I know you, honey."

She started the car, her legs shaking. "I think you're making too much of it. We are *friends*. That's all." Liar, liar, pants on fire.

Sarah drove the last few blocks in silence, her mind all over the place as she tried to sort out her feelings. Why was she attracted to Franco? He wasn't her type.

It didn't matter, she decided firmly as she pulled into

the empty parking lot at the warehouse. The feelings couldn't go anywhere. She wouldn't let them, for Bella's sake. Someday Franco would fall in love with someone who could be a mother, the perfect wife.

With the right pedigree. The right background. *Not me.*

She and her mom put away the crates, greeting Nashville who didn't budge from her bed by the window. "Are you sure you want to come in on your day off?"

"I love it here," Jennifer said. "It's quiet and I get to read or play with the animals. Nashville actually sits on my lap when you aren't around."

"Really?" The cat was contrary, no doubt about it.

"Yep."

"Well, we just have the bunny, the iguana and that black Tom left." She shrugged. "But it can change so quickly. One phone call is all it takes and we could be back to a full house."

As if she willed it to happen, her phone rang. Sharing a smile with her mother, Sarah shrugged and answered. "Pet Rescue, how can we help you today?"

She listened as the man she'd given the ticket to for the barking dog yelled so loudly her mom could hear it from where she stood.

"Yes, sir. You have to pay the ticket. As you'll see, I left you literature on ways to keep your dog happy while you aren't home. I realize you work full time."

Sarah winced as the man went through every swear

word he knew before finally telling her to come get the dog before he let it loose, then he hung up.

"Want to go for a ride, Mom?"

"I don't think it is safe, Sarah. What if he attacks you?"

"That doesn't happen in real life. That poor animal! If his owner has such a short temper, what do you think we'll find?" People could be so cruel to animals that relied solely on human kindness.

"I'll have the cops on speed dial," her mom decided, determination in the set of her shoulders.

"I have my taser. In the glove box."

"Sarah. Is that even legal?"

"For self-defense purposes. I have the civilian version and a permit, anyway."

Her mom nodded, her mouth grim. "Let's go."

They got back into the truck together, tension thick.

Sarah thought of all the things that could go wrong. "Maybe you should stay here, Mom…"

"I'm going." Her mom clamped onto the inside of the passenger seat. "How far is it?"

"Five minutes. But you'll be surprised at the change in scenery." It amazed her that such a beautiful, rich place could have pockets of poverty.

Sarah slowly pulled up in front of the forlorn looking house. Decrepit, unpainted steps leading to a buckled porch. The front door was wide open, a dog the size of a chocolate lab chained to the pillar. Of course, it was barking.

A neighbor saw Sarah arrive and high-tailed it out of her own house as Sarah selected supplies from the back of her truck. This lady had seen better days, if her satin robe was anything to go by. Grown-out dyed blonde hair and a cigarette dangling from her lip completed her downgrade.

"You just missed 'im, the bastard." She flicked her ash to the street and kept the cigarette clamped firmly between her fingers. "Took off without payin' his rent. Damn dog won't stop barkin', can't sleep, can't have company over. Can't hear the TV."

Sarah smiled in commiseration, not wanting to go for any more details of the woman's life. "Did he say where?" If the dog was hurt...

"Probably Georgia. He got family there." The woman took a deep drag of her cigarette, and squinted against the light. "My man wants to shut this dog up, got it?" She drew her finger across her throat.

"That won't be necessary." Sarah's stomach sank and anger welled inside her. She walked toward the porch and the miserable animal. It wasn't his fault his owner had been irresponsible. She could count his ribs and saw sores along his back. Resolve gave her courage and she turned her back on the woman to face the dog. "I'm here. I've got this now."

She felt her mother come up at her side as she studied the growling animal. "Do you need treats? A muzzle?

You don't know what this dog has, honey." Sarah hadn't heard her mom so quietly furious in a very long time. "It's good he went back to Georgia, that man. I want to wring his neck."

Sarah stood at the bottom step, feeling sorry for the dog as it lunged at her, scared and angry. "It's all right, pooch," she crooned, tears in her eyes. She pulled the thick gloves from her back pocket and slipped them on. "Mom, could you get a bowl from the back and fill it with water? I've got a jug next to a baggie of dog food. Bring that too."

"Whatchya gonna do?" the woman asked, coughing into her fist as she flicked her cigarette butt to the dead grass in the front yard.

"Take care of him," Sarah said, doing her best not to judge. It wasn't easy, but she focused on what she could fix. The dog. Part Pit Bull and part Lab, he had a stocky, barrel-shaped body and a strong jaw. His eyes were wild with fear and as she put her foot on the bottom stair, the dog winced and lunged.

She wanted to pull the dog in for a hug, but he'd tear her head off.

"Here, Sarah," her mom said, joining her on the bottom step. "Water and food."

"The chain is really short. He can't reach that far. I'm going to climb over the rail and meet him on the porch. Skip the stairs."

"Be careful!"

Sarah pulled herself up and over, landing on the porch with a thunk that made the dog go crazy. "It's all right," Sarah sang. "I know I'm in your territory, but I just want to help. Okay?"

Her mom handed her the water dish, which Sarah slid across the wood to the dog. He eyed the water, but wouldn't stop barking long enough to drink.

"You don't have to be afraid of me." Sarah sat down, her back against the side of the house, letting the dog get used to her. To realize she wasn't a threat.

Ten minutes passed and the barks slowed then at last stopped. Sarah, who had been looking at the sky and counting clouds while thinking of ways to make Georgia pay for his cruelty, heard the sloppy slurps of a thirsty dog.

Slowly, she rolled food his way a few nuggets at a time. She inched closer as he ate until she was able to feed him from her gloved hand. Sarah quickly attached the muzzle over him. He snapped and she jumped back but she didn't let go.

Crooning to him as she pet him, Sarah wanted to let him know he was safe. The dog shook with nerves as he panted, his eyes wild. He growled low in his chest. "I won't hurt you, okay?"

The dog trembled. Barked in warning.

"Careful, Sarah," her mom said, standing by the porch.

"I know." She slowly got up, attached a chest

harness and a leash, and led the dog down the stairs.

The neighbor, who'd stayed to watch the entire thing while smoking two more cigarettes, huffed. "Never heard that dog quiet before."

"Have a nice day," Sarah said as politely as she could. Her entire body was jumping with adrenalin. Sorrow, righteous anger and nowhere to put it. She coaxed the dog into the back of the truck, securing him a kennel.

He was calm now, but shivering with fear of the unknown.

Sarah got in the truck, shut the door and blinked tears from her eyes. Her mom said, "What are we going to do with him?"

"I'm going to get him set up at the warehouse," she said. "He needs a bath and check-up before I can integrate him with the others."

"Are you sure, Sarah? He could be really dangerous."

"Mom, it's what I do. The whole point of Pet Rescue is dogs like him." Unwanted. Abused. "I think he'll be fine after a day or two. An air-conditioned warehouse with room to run and food and water will be like heaven."

"Nobody yelling at him. Beating him." Her mom clenched her fists against her denim-clad thighs.

"He's safe now, Mom."

"I have never been more proud of you, Sarah. But I was this close," she put her fingers together an inch apart, "to punching that woman in the face."

Chapter Thirteen

Franco arrived at Pet Rescue at 7:00 on the dot, eager to see Sarah. He told himself the anticipation in his veins had everything to do with getting new stock for the pet store and nothing to do with a certain blonde with golden skin.

Today he brought his 458 Italia Ferrari he used when he wasn't driving the Volvo and Bella around. There was nothing quite like opening up on the road, full throttle. He had the tickets to prove it.

Going inside, he was greeted by yipping and then a loud growling that didn't sound like it came from the toy

Pom or the Chihuahua. He scowled, took off his Armani sunglasses and blinked into the room.

Jennifer Murphy had hold of an angry dark brown dog the size of a pony, a pinch collar around its gigantic neck. Benny and Pippa yapped from behind their barricade in the kitchen.

"Quiet, Buster," Jennifer said.

Franco put his hand to his chest. "Me?" He'd never been called Buster in his life.

"No." Jennifer shook her head, her hair in a clip and springing curls all over. "This is our newest rescue."

"Good luck finding a home," he said. "Even I would have a tough time there. He looks ready to kill."

"He might not be so fond of men," Jennifer said with a nod and a pat on the dog's head. "His owner was a real jerk. We're keeping Buster separate from the other animals until Dr. Wilton gives him the okay. Then we'll see. I have an idea he'll settle in."

"Is Sarah ready?" Franco looked around, walking toward the kitchen so he could give Benny and Pippa a pat. Coffee brewed in a Mr. Coffee 12-cup machine—a far cry from the Brazilian blend he made at home.

"She's in the warehouse. Buster here didn't like his bedding, so he tore it up rather than sleep on it. She'll just be a second."

Sarah pushed through the door connecting the office to the warehouse. "Done. No more cushy foam for him. I put in the straw pallet. Maybe that will be more his style."

She looked up and blushed as she saw Franco. "Oh. Hi. I thought I was talking to my mom."

"Morning," he said, his mood lifting at her smile. "I was just hearing about Buster."

"He's going to need some work, but we can talk about it in the car. Did you eat breakfast? I've got granola bars somewhere."

"I figured we could get coffee on the way out of town."

"Perfect, since I didn't have time for that either." She gestured to the beige shorts and soft yellow silk shirt she wore. "I was trying to blend, but now I smell like dog."

Franco looked down, seeing that Sarah didn't bother painting her toes. She wore sandals with two slick yellow straps that showed off narrow feet.

"I don't think that will be a problem where we are going."

She grinned. "The breeders? Probably not."

He sniffed her. "You smell great to me."

"Sweet talker." She brushed by him without meeting his gaze, careful not to touch him. "Mom. We're leaving. The truck keys are on the counter in the kitchen. Martin will be in to walk Buster later, okay? Call me if you need anything!"

She grabbed her purse, a soft leather pouch with embroidered trim. The bohemian style suited her. It seemed more natural than the khakis and polo shirt.

"Have fun! Drive safe, Mr. de Silva." Jennifer

Murphy pointed her finger at him. "And good luck with the chi-poo."

Laughing, Jennifer sank back in the office chair, her hand still holding Buster's collar.

Sarah pushed out the front door. "She is having way too much fun."

"What is the matter with that?"

"She wants to help me, which is great, but I need to do this myself."

"You said that yesterday, too," Franco reminded her, opening the passenger door of his car for her. "There is nothing wrong with accepting a helping hand."

She stared at his car and then looked at him. "Now and then," Sarah agreed, grinning as she patted the top of the car. "Shiny. Black. The only reason I know it's a Ferrari is because my cousin watches Top Gear. You must be the most popular dad at Bella's school."

"I drive the Volvo when Bella is with me. I don't get behind the wheel of this one as often as I'd like." He waited by the door as she slid in against the decadent leather seats.

Sarah sighed with appreciation. "This is smooth, Franco."

He thought she was smooth, showing her tanned thighs as her shorts slid up. The soft lemon silky blouse settled around her, her long hair straight and falling past her shoulders in a smooth curtain. She reached for the door to close it, just as he shut it from the outside.

Independent, he thought, going around to the driver's side. Franco got in, the sleek car purring to life. "Coffee?"

"I'm all right for now. Maybe once we've been on the road a while."

"Sure."

"Pretty much I don't want to spill anything in your car."

"It washes." She was sweet to think of that.

"Was Bella terribly upset that she couldn't come?"

"She'd forgotten all about it, actually. My daughter likes school. Can you believe it?"

Sarah laughed. "Uh-oh. You might have a geek on your hands. I liked school too."

"You're very smart." He kept both hands on the steering wheel, even though her bare skin was close enough to touch. Tempting.

"Focused. It's different. I had to study. A lot. But I wanted to. I thought I might be a vet, but changed my mind two years into the program. I wanted to find homes for the unwanted animals, not just know how to stitch them up. Which I can do, by the way. School wasn't wasted."

Franco pulled onto I-95. "Learning and expanding the mind is rarely a bad thing."

Silence settled for a few moments. Franco stole glances at Sarah, who looked out the window at the passing cars. He liked that she didn't feel the need to chatter. Fill up the conversation.

"It doesn't even feel like we're moving." Sarah brushed her hand over the dash. "We could be flying, it drives so smooth."

"I have to be careful of speeding," Franco acknowledged. "It's easy to do. I get lost in thought and the next thing I know…"

She smiled, glancing at the speedometer. "I'll help you keep watch. So. What else do you know about this breeder? Have you bought from them before?"

"No." Franco gestured to the portfolio by her feet. "But go ahead and read about them. The Brownings are new so there aren't any bad reviews."

"No good reviews either," Sarah said.

"True. Which is why we're making the trip to check these puppies out."

She opened the folder and scanned the information. "The American Canine Hybrid Club calls it a chi-poo, but," she looked at him with a disbelieving laugh. "It's also known as a choodle. People are so strange."

"What else does it say?"

"Toy breed, 5 to 10 pounds. Requires grooming. Good for condo living. Sociable."

Franco nodded. "It's the condo living that makes it an easy sell. Unlike your Buster. What happened there?"

Sarah rested her head back against the seat and closed her eyes, frowning. "A guy who decided to head back to Georgia did his dog a favor and left him behind."

She sat up and faced him, crossing her legs. “I don’t understand how people can be so cruel to something that offers unconditional love.”

He heard the anger she barely suppressed. “Lucky dog, to have gotten you.”

“One county over, and he would probably be put down,” Sarah said. “I’m the only no-kill facility here.”

“Now what will happen?”

“I have to get Buster used to people, his shots and a check up with Dr. Wilton. He’s already fixed.” Sarah tilted her head. “See what his temperament is, though he didn’t seem interested in my two yappers, that’s no guarantee he’ll be sweet with other animals. He likes my mom.”

Franco laughed. “Who wouldn’t?”

“I’m just saying. We have to wait and see. It’s easier with puppies and kittens. They’re tiny and cute and don’t have strong personalities yet.”

“Buster needs a home full of football players or something.”

Sarah lifted her hand as if to stop his words. “I don’t know about that. He might do better with a single woman, someone he can protect. A single man? It would have to be a special guy to get beyond what Georgia did.”

“Is there any recourse, legally, for you to follow up on?”

“I’d given him a ticket before, and warned him if it happened again he’d have to go to court. There are laws against animal cruelty." She tapped her fingers along the folder. "I gave him literature on how to help keep his dog from barking."

"You can't save everybody, Sarah. People have to want to change." He thought of Bianca and changed the subject. "I'd like to buy one of the puppies to bring back to Dr. Wilton for a complete examination."

"Smart idea. She is amazing. Genuinely cares about what she does."

"Like you. Here's the exit that switches out to Sawgrass. Coffee?"

"I'm really fine," she said. "We'll be there in no time."

Franco liked driving, liked having Sarah with him in the intimacy of the car. "So, tell me about you." Unable to resist, he reached over to touch her hand and she jolted. She was not immune to him, he noticed happily, so he left his hand over hers.

"Uh, what do you want to know?" She gave a nervous laugh. "I love food, the ocean and I'm a Pisces."

"Married?"

"I ended an engagement because we didn't agree on *my* career path."

"What does that mean?"

"He was a vet, and wanted me to be a vet too. I had my own ideas about the pet rescue I wanted to start instead, and he told me I'd fail. No money in the non-profit business. Which he was right about, but money is not what motivates me."

"You aren't failing." He had a million ideas to help her but he was glad he kept quiet about them. He'd only known her a few months and knew that money was not what drove her. "Look at all of the animals you've found homes for."

"Thanks. He had a list of ways I could be successful and use my education so that it wasn't a 'waste'." She cleared her throat. "He expected me to take a break, raise kids, and work in our veterinarian office together. I like kids, but I wasn't ready to pop them out by some graph he'd made up." She shrugged. "And now? I'm thirty."

"Thirty is not too old to start a family. These days, people wait until they're forty. They have their career first, then settle down. In a way, it makes more sense. You have financial stability, you've grown up yourself, and you've sowed your wild oats."

Sarah leaned against the passenger door, adjusting her upper body so she could see him better. She didn't pull her hand away. He winked.

"I didn't have any wild oats." She lifted her shoulder. "But I have no regrets. My job matters, and there is plenty of drama to keep me from feeling too boring. The ocean keeps me sane after a rough day."

"You are *not* boring." Franco switched lanes to avoid a carnival on wheels that was part of a long fair caravan headed west. "You have a full life, doing what you love." Some folks searched for that their entire life without finding it.

"True." She patted her chest with her free hand. "I'm not against having someone important in my life, but they'd have to understand that I'm my own person."

"I appreciate that. I've been learning so much about myself this last year," Franco said. "Being the sole person in charge of another human being's welfare set me back on my heels. But I wouldn't change a minute. I feel like Bella has made me better, more well-rounded. And a little bit paranoid," he added, laughing.

"You are an amazing dad."

"Thank you." He squeezed her hand and brought the subject back to her. "I can't stop thinking about our kiss. About you. I remember how beautiful you were, coming from the ocean like a goddess. Water droplets shining on your tanned skin, your eyes green as the sea."

She tugged her hand free, embarrassed. "Attraction. I'm betting you haven't done too much dating since your wife died."

"There have been a few." He wasn't a monk, for God's sake. "Nothing serious."

"I feel as if we are becoming such good friends. I don't want to ruin that. And Bella doesn't need to be confused."

Friends, again? "How would Bella be confused?"

"Well, I'd be around, and then, when our *desire* ran its course, I wouldn't be." She looked out the window and then back again. "I really care about her."

"First of all, I cannot believe you are using Bella to turn me away, and second of all, just how quickly do you think our desire would fade?" He'd never had this instant, or deep, of a connection before.

Her poor cheeks turned so red they looked painful. "You're a man of the world, Franco. I don't know. I'm just a South Florida girl on a mission."

"You don't give yourself enough credit." He had been around, around enough to appreciate a treasure when he found it.

"We are in separate zip codes."

Americans! "We have the same zip code. 33308."

Exasperated, she twisted her hair around her finger and tied it in a bun at the back of her head. "You are mega rich. I am forced to sell dog treats at a car wash to get the roof fixed. How long do you think we could last?"

"Sarah, if you had all the money in the world, what would you do?" She was so fortunate, already living her dream.

"Get my roof fixed?"

"Seriously."

"I'd..." She tapped her lower lip. "I would do the same thing I'm doing now, but I would expand. Help more animals."

"I can help you do that."

"But that's my point! You helping me do it means that I wouldn't be doing it, and that takes away some of the joy for me. The satisfaction of knowing I did it myself."

"I don't care about how much money you have or don't have. I just want to help, because I like you. Those treats you created taste wonderful. I know a marketing guy who can take them to the next level. I am not offering anything other than a contact. A name. You do the rest."

She sighed and stretched her legs out in front of her. "Just let me think about it, okay?" Sarah hummed beneath her breath and closed her eyes for a few minutes then she sat up and looked at him. "Your turn to share a story. Tell me about your wildest escapade. Before you got married, settled down and turned boring. I mean, respectable."

Franco grinned. "Well, I was born on the Amazon. My family lived in a village there…"

"A village? Why am I not buying that you grew up in a poor little rainforest town eating grubs?"

"So maybe my family owned the village," he conceded, sending her a smile.

Sarah hated to admit it, but she was well and truly charmed by Franco de Silva. He drove the car like it was an extension of himself. Confident, sexy. Why did he keep touching her? Why did she let him hold her hand?

He made it really hard to stick to that *just friends* thing she kept telling herself. She listened to his mesmerizing voice as he talked of his childhood, the love for his family clear. God, his voice was such a turn on. Lightly accented, deep. Rich. Perfect.

"Where are they now?" she asked. "Your family?"

"They're gone. Dead. Life is a precious thing and the trail of loved ones behind me reminds me every day." His jaw clenched.

He wore the dark shadows well, combining grief with hope in a way that spoke to her heart. "My dad left us when I was thirteen. I didn't have any brothers or sisters; it had always been just the three of us. I had cousins, of course—Mom's brothers. Mom worked in an office, Dad fished. I'm pretty sure the only reason my folks got married was because of me. Well, Mom getting pregnant."

"They did the right thing." Franco made the question a statement.

"I don't know..." Sarah looked inward. "They never seemed happy. It was a relief when Dad left, which is sad, I think."

"Is he remarried?"

"Yeah. Ten years ago he married this girl in the Keys. She's my age. I don't call her Mom, if you know what I mean."

Franco didn't laugh, but offered his hand again. Sarah took it, caressing his fingers. "I'm sorry," he said. "I know what it's like to be disappointed by those we love."

"I looked up your wife, after our dinner the other

night," she confessed.

"You did?" Now Franco chuckled. "The late, great Bianca Rodrigues?"

"Yes. She was beautiful."

"Rotten on the inside. Spoiled fruit."

Sarah tightened her grip on his hand. "It must have been hard, dealing with all of the paparazzi. There were so many stories, I couldn't even begin to read them all. And the images of Bella..."

Franco cursed. "I tried so hard to get those removed from public view. Bianca's fans wanted to see Bella's grief. It sickened me. The day I punched a reporter was the day I realized I had to get out of Bahia. South Florida has always called to me."

"So I Googled Bahia," she said, letting her voice trail before she laughed.

"I like that you are curious about me." He caressed her thumb with his, their fingers joined.

"It's so old there," she said. "The buildings on the water look ready to fall in. You have a history that I don't have."

"A lot of history. A lot of drama. Here it is quieter, and peaceful. It's good for the soul to have time to reflect. Not that I don't like a good party every once in a while. The older I get, the longer I can go between them." He flashed a grin that made her skin heat.

"I don't care about parties," she said. He was far from old.

"You've never partied with the Brazilians. We dance, sing and eat. So much food. I learned from the older chefs the value of simplicity. Letting the flavors of the fruits and vegetables, the fish or meat, speak." He pinched his fingers together and made a kissing noise. "I will take you to Bahia, if you'd like."

Sarah laughed. "I'm busy today."

"I can make a few phone calls. We could leave this afternoon." He brought her knuckles up to his mouth and kissed them, just that light brush of his mouth made her suck in her stomach. "I will not bore you with fizzling desire."

He thought she would be bored? Heaven help her. "Franco." Then she clamped her mouth closed.

If he wanted to think of her as some hot Lolita type, who was she to argue?

"I think this is our exit."

He nodded, signaling and then moving over. "I've got a small crate folded behind your seat, if we find one that we like. We'd have to drive home with it at your feet."

"Hmm." She saw plenty she liked, all right.

Driving the Ferrari like a rock star.

Just. Friends.

Chapter Fourteen

They left the highway and turned into a rural area. She scanned the side of the road until she saw a large green sign. “Turn here,” Sarah said. “Browning Puppies. We made it without seeing a single alligator.”

“Thank God.” He tapped the steering wheel with his thumb and leaned toward the sign as they passed. “Melissa and Eric Browning.” Franco drove slowly down the dirt road. “Next time, you should drive. In your truck. This is going to ruin my alignment.”

Next time? “Can you get on the grass?” The luxury

automobile wasn't made for back-country driving.

"I see the house at the end." Franco winced as they hit a pothole.

They parked on the gravel square before a sprawling house built around 1970. Single story. Separate garage and a barn area where a cow grazed. A small vegetable garden struggled under the hot sun, but it seemed well-tended.

"Nothing flashy," Sarah observed out loud. It was a good start.

Franco and Sarah walked up the five stairs to the white concrete porch. Franco knocked, but the door was already being opened.

"Mr. de Silva," the woman, maybe late twenties, greeted them and pushed open the screened door. She had a baby on her hip, and a toddler screaming behind her as she looked at Sarah. "Ma'am."

"My wife," Franco said smoothly as he took her hand.

Sarah coughed to cover her surprise and discretely pinched his thumb. "Pleased to meet you."

"Excuse the chaos. There just isn't as much time in the day as I'd like to get it all done, you know? Kids, housework, and with both of our mama's giving birth at the same time, well, you can just imagine the stress level around here!"

Mrs. Browning set the baby in a playpen, handed a cracker to the crying child, and wiped her hands on a paper towel after washing them in the kitchen.

Sarah did her best to keep smiling, but it took all she had to stay put and not run for the front door and Franco's get-away car. This was domestic bliss?

"Honey!" The woman poked her head into a bedroom or office off to the side of the hall. "Can you come out here a sec? We've got a couple that wants to see the puppies." She stepped back as her husband came out of the room.

Dark brown hair lay flat against his head, his clothes were rumpled, but Mr. Browning had a welcoming smile that put Sarah at ease. "Nice to meet you. I'm Eric. You've met Melissa?"

"Sorry," his wife said in a rush. "I forgot to introduce myself. These days I'm lucky to remember my name."

"No problem," Franco said, his charm in full force as he shook Eric's hand. "I've been looking forward to seeing this chi-poo. The pictures you sent are nice, but it's hard to tell for sure if it's what my wife is looking for until we see them up close."

Sarah swore vengeance beneath her breath but smiled to the Brownings. "Personality. It all depends on personality. What made you decide to start breeding puppies?"

"Melissa's family has always had toy Poodles, but we saw a chi-poo in a pet store and fell in love. Melissa and I had one toy Poodle, Missy, already."

"So there are two moms?" Sarah asked. That would

explain why there were so many puppies.

"Yes." Eric scraped a hand across his stubble chin. "We bought a long hair female Chihuahua, and decided to see what we could come up with."

"Experimenting." Sarah wasn't sure how she felt about that, but then, how else would you discover what worked best?

"We decided to get both mamas pregnant at the same time and just get it done all at once." Melissa tugged her little boy close, sticky fingers from his cracker and all. "There is something to be said about getting it over with." She chuckled and covered her barely bulging belly with her free hand.

Sarah smiled, hoping it wasn't a grimace. Three babies. And puppies? This had serious madhouse potential.

"I work from home, website stuff." Eric slipped his arm around Melissa's waist. "The puppies will bring in enough money so that Melissa can stay home too and we don't need to worry about daycare. It's more hectic than a traditional nine to five, but we answer to ourselves. I like that."

"Us, too," Franco said, giving Sarah a doting expression. "Not that there isn't a headache in owning your own business. However, we've found that the rewards outweigh the hard times."

Sarah tugged on his arm before he told the couple too much. She had to know if they were treating the dogs well.

They practically admitted they were doing it for the money.

Most reputable breeders started out in the business because they had a favorite puppy and they wanted to raise more of them. This couple shared they were looking at the bottom line. It didn't mean they were wrong, but Sarah wanted to make sure they weren't skimping on food or supplies to make ends meet.

"Where are the puppies?"

"We've got the back room set up for them. Moms and babies. Follow me," Eric said.

Melissa picked up the toddler and settled the little boy on her hip. He stuck his thumb in his mouth and stared at her and Franco with wide brown eyes. "He's shy," Melissa said, brushing his wispy hair back off his forehead.

"He's sweet," Sarah said, marveling at how kids could be so clingy, but cute. She hadn't lied when she said she'd felt no ticking biological clock, but something tugged at her heart strings as she watched the maternal kiss Melissa placed on her son's head.

"Are you coming?" Franco asked, his eyes narrowed as he watched her watch Melissa. "The puppies are this way. I can hear them."

"Yes, of course."

He held out his hand and Sarah took it, knowing if she didn't it would look weird. Franco would owe her for the marriage remarks. *Married to Franco?* She couldn't even imagine it.

"Missy is a black toy Poodle, Farrah is a long hair Chihuahua, brown and white. The puppies are assorted."

"Do you have any black puppies?" Bella had requested one, Sarah remembered.

"Yes. More Poodle looking than Chihuahua. When they were born they looked like guinea pigs, but they're cuter now." Eric opened the door to a back bedroom that had windows on two sides, the temperature controlled by a separate unit on the wall.

"This is really nice," she said, glancing at Franco.

"We keep it at 78 degrees. The kids aren't allowed back here so that the puppies can rest. We've tried to make it as sterile as possible."

The room was clean, the puppy training pads in two places on the thin outdoor carpeted flooring. There were two large open crates that made it seem like a den for each mama. It must have been feeding time, since both mothers had a line of babies at her belly.

"Do they switch off?" Franco asked. His hair curled at his neck, his brow furrowed in curiosity. "Brothers and sisters?"

"Every once in a while, we get a crossover, but for the most part, they stick with their mom and littermates." Eric leaned down to pick up a white and black puppy with tufts of hair. Mostly Chihuahua but with a larger Poodle nose, it was cute. "This guy likes to travel. The moms don't mind, surprisingly enough."

"How old are they?" Sarah asked, remembering that the file said six weeks.

"Six weeks, three days," Eric answered, tucking the little guy next to his siblings. "We can't release them until 8 weeks old. It isn't the ideal situation, unless you already have pets at home?"

Sarah shook her head, appreciating his integrity. "What do you recommend? With no other pets."

"Eight weeks at the earliest. Nine would be better. We can get a start on potty training here. Would you be walking them?"

"Condo living. We have a piece of grass but it isn't fenced." Franco eyed the two different litters. "They look really healthy. The mamas seem happy, too."

"They're pure hybrids. I mean, both the parents for each are registered full breeds with the AKC." Eric scooted a straggler back to the others. "If that matters to you, or not. We're asking 1000.00 per puppy, which includes shots and a veterinary visit of your choice. If there is anything the matter, we will exchange the puppy or give you a refund."

Franco rocked back on his heels. "You seem sure of your puppies."

Sarah hid her surprise, keeping her eyes on the roly-poly fur-babies. That was an excellent guarantee.

She lifted her head as Eric spoke. "We've been using a local vet." Eric seemed way too young to have a puppy farm and a million kids. "He's really taught us a lot, approving the studs we used."

Sarah nodded, impressed. Once a year wasn't a lot of money, but it beat paying daycare. And the couple seemed to care, if this back room was anything to judge by.

Would Eric get greedy and try to breed the dogs too quickly? Sarah thought of how to ask the question without sounding too much like, well, an animal control officer.

Franco came to her rescue. "When will you have more puppies?"

"The vet says they should only have puppies once a year, and only three times for a life span. But by then, Melissa wants to go back to school and finish her degree. She's going to be a teacher."

"Sounds like a plan," Franco said.

Sarah nodded. They were doing it right, anyway. If Dr. Wilton signed off on them, she would feel good recommending the Brownings and their chi-poos. "Can I hold the black one?"

Eric leaned down and picked up the puppy. "Sure. Do you feel her calling to you?"

"I don't know about that," Sarah said, smiling. The last thing she wanted was another pet. "But she's pretty darn cute." Black eyes, button nose, little pink tongue. Puppies had a new smell that couldn't be bottled. They brought an instant feeling of warmth and love.

Why was she feeling so sappy?

The puppy licked her cheek, tail wagging with excitement. Sarah's heart filled. Maybe one more dog wouldn't be terrible...she met Franco's mysterious gaze. What would it be like to have a man like him in her life?

A warm trickle over Sarah's hand brought her back to the moment. She looked for the closest pee pad and set the puppy down.

Franco's chest heaved with silent laughter.

Eric's throat turned red and he led Sarah to a small sink in the attached bathroom. "Sorry about that. Hazard of the trade, I think."

Sarah washed up, laughing at herself for thinking she and Franco made a good team. Franco looked good. Mr. Cool and Charming. She was a disaster. *As usual.*

Franco wore a neutral expression and had his hands behind his back as she came out of the bathroom. "Does that little darling have your name on it?"

Sarah shook her head. It would serve him right if she said yes. How would he like an untrained puppy loose on his leather seats?

"Let's talk about it on the way home, *honey*." She brushed by him toward the door Eric held open.

"If you can't decide, we can take them all. I want you to be happy."

Was that his signal that he wanted them for the business? Or just how he operated? Can't decide on one—so take them all? Sarah sniffed. Money did not buy everything. She should ask for them, right now. His seats would be ruined. Married. Happy. *Really?*

Eric followed them out, shutting the door behind

them. "Well, if you decide, let us know. You seem like real nice people."

Franco hooked his arm through Sarah's. "I think we'd like the black one."

They stopped again in the kitchen, where Melissa had the baby in a high chair. The toddler sat at the table eating a banana dipped in peanut butter. Melissa wore an apron around her middle and stirred something delicious on the stove.

Eric went over and smelled the soup pot. "I can't wait for lunch. You two want to stay and join us?"

Franco's nose was slightly flared as if he could separate the spices from the air. "We have to get back to the city, but may I ask what you are making?"

Melissa's cheeks flushed. "Vegetable beef stew, that's all. Nothing fancy, but we grow our own tomatoes and onions."

"It reminds me of my mother's soup," Franco said.

Sarah knew Franco could buy and sell this couple's farm ten times over, but he was sincere in his compliments and not the least bit judgmental. She liked that about him.

Sarah had to admit that she liked a lot of things about him.

"I make a mean corn muffin," Eric said.

Franco took his wallet from his back pocket. "I'd like to put a deposit down on the black puppy. We can come get her in the next two weeks?"

Eric exchanged a glance with his wife. "You don't

have to put a deposit down. We'll hold her for you."

"Which one did you choose?" Melissa asked. She handed the baby in the high chair another small piece of banana. From what Sarah could tell, the baby preferred putting it in her hair rather than eating any of it.

"They like Farrah's all black one."

"Oh yes," Melissa said with an agreeable nod, "she's pretty."

Sarah was starting to feel bad about not being honest with this couple. They seemed very nice. "We should go, Franco. And let these people get on with their day."

Franco nodded, setting five hundred dollars on the counter. "I'll be in touch. So the mom is the Chihuahua, and the sire is the Poodle?"

"Yes," Eric said, walking them toward the front door as Sarah waved good-bye to the kids. "Black."

They stepped out to the porch and the gleaming Ferrari in the sunshine. Eric looked from Franco to Sarah and asked, "What do you do, again?"

Chapter Fifteen

Franco burst out laughing as soon as they reached the highway. "You should have seen the look on your face when that puppy peed on you."

"And you think that's funny?" Sarah rolled her eyes and sat back against the leather seat. "Nice husband you are. What was that all about, anyway? A little warning would have been good. I thought I was going to scream."

"Being married to me would make you scream?" He studied her profile as she stared straight ahead, her mouth lifting in a reluctant smile. He never thought he'd even *joke* about marriage again. Seeing the Brownings in action made him realize what he'd been missing. What he'd expected from his own marriage but had been lacking all along.

"Don't take it personally," Sarah said. "And three kids under the age of four? What are they thinking?"

"It is no accident," Franco observed, having secretly enjoyed the rising panic in Sarah as she realized Melissa was pregnant. Not much shook Sarah. "She's going to be a teacher. They breed puppies. They know what they're doing."

"The sign did say they were professional breeders." Sarah smacked her palm against the door and snickered. "I just didn't realize they were putting it to practice."

"I liked them." Franco checked the rearview mirror, then the side mirror before switching lanes. "Are you hungry? It would have been rude, yes, to stay for lunch? Though the soup smelled good. Fresh ingredients make all the difference."

"We could have had a taste. I don't think they would have minded." Sarah smoothed her hands down her bare shins. "Did you see that baby with the banana?"

He'd seen Sarah shudder as she avoided getting too close to the high chair. Chuckling, Franco asked, "Are you sure you don't want to have a dozen babies?"

"No." Sarah's face paled beneath her golden tan. "My job keeps me way too busy. Emotionally draining and all of that. That house was chaos!"

Franco would bet big money that Sarah Murphy had the maternal gene waiting dormant inside her. Even if she didn't want to admit it. "How about lunch?"

Sarah put her hand to her stomach. "Sounds good. What are you in the mood for?"

You, he thought. *And anything that allows me to be close to you.* "Italian? I know a place on the way back."

"Sure," she agreed with a shrug. "I'm not picky."

She wasn't. From what Franco had seen of Sarah, she was easy-going, unless there was an animal involved, and then her fighting gloves came on. She enjoyed her life and didn't let the hard knocks keep her down.

"I found this restaurant by accident," Franco said, signaling to get off the highway. "When I was picking up a batch of Maltese puppies. I ended up with a flat tire because the roads weren't paved. Well, I'll let you be the judge of the pasta. I hope the place is still there." Franco rested his hand on the bare skin just above her knee, unable to resist touching her. Despite the hot day, her skin was cool thanks to the air conditioning in his car.

"Me, too." Sarah swallowed audibly and refused to look at him. She didn't shove his hand away, which he took as a good sign. She needed to get used to him touching her...he'd take it slow, he thought with a smile.

Franco turned on the program in the car, asking for the address to La Vida Loca.

"You're taking me to The Crazy Life?" Sarah turned toward him as she asked the question, one dimple flashing.

"My life is crazy enough, my friend."

"I did not choose the name. The woman who owns the place married an Italian who taught her everything she knows. She's from the swamps, she said."

"The swamps? Like, Louisiana?"

"No, no," Franco said, turning into the dirt parking lot. A red building with faded paint, white-trimmed windows and a neon sign beckoned. "The Cypress Swamp."

"A woman from the local swamp makes the best pasta you've ever had?"

"Maybe not the best, but very good. The sign says it's still open." He'd had mussels steamed in wine tossed with homemade pasta. It seemed simple, but it had been amazing.

Not as amazing as kissing Sarah, which was the bar everything else came to these days. The car ride, intimate, and getting to know one another, the pretending to be husband and wife—it got to him. And he knew she felt it too, which made it doubly hard to deny or resist.

The fact that she thought they were only friends?

Insanity.

He parked, turned to Sarah and leaned across the console to kiss her.

Startled, she kissed him back, pressing her lips against his mouth with a small hum at the back of her throat. The heat between them flared to life and it was all he could do to stay on his side of the damned car.

Screw it.

He unbuckled his seat belt, pushed the car seat back so he could get out from behind the wheel. Impatient, wanting her closer, he knelt over the console and cupped the back of her head in his palm.

Her eyes turned dark green with desire, which amped his need higher until he thought he might combust.

"Franco?" She lightly wet her lips with her tongue as if nervous beneath his gaze.

"We are not friends, *querida*. How many times must I tell you this? I want you, Sarah." He brought her gently to him, then captured her mouth in a searing kiss. He caressed her bare arm, felt her unhook her seat belt as she too perched on her knees in the front seat of his car.

It wasn't level and she slipped back with a soft laugh.

"Somehow I never imagined making out with you in the front seat of your car."

Franco pulled back a few inches, their noses a hair's breadth apart. "It's been a while, yes. I am not going to apologize."

She brought her hand up to the back of his neck, trying to find balance. "For kissing me?"

"For wanting you."

"I don't want you to be sorry. I've never felt like this." She tickled her fingers across his jaw. "I knew when I first saw you, dark and handsome, that you would kiss like the devil himself. Your mouth is pure temptation." She spoke, their mouths almost touching.

"You thought I was tempting? Even when you gave me the citation?" He dropped his hand to the curve of her hip. "I've heard of giving someone flowers to show how you feel, but never a ticket. It must be an American tradition." Franco tugged her closer.

Sarah gently nipped his lower lip. "I didn't want to let you off the hook just because you're sexy."

Franco grinned. "You think I'm sexy?"

She nodded, her cheeks turning pink as she stared into his eyes. "Unbelievably hot." She trailed her tongue across the spot she'd nipped and his blood fired.

"You're a goddess," he said, his voice deep.

Sarah laughed. "Flesh and blood woman." She leaned into his caress as he followed the dip of her waist. "Don't get your expectations too high."

He pulled her up and into his arms, wrapping her tightly in his embrace. They fell backward into his front seat, the position not one for comfort.

She landed on top of him, her eyes sparkling with mischief as she placed her hands on either side of his face, her lower half hovering over his very evident ardor. "I think we should go in and order lunch." She skimmed her hand over the hard ridge straining against his jeans, teasing. "Then we can think about dessert. Back at my house."

Franco, feeling as frustrated as a hormonal teenager, stole one last kiss, ramping up the heat so that her eyes crossed. "I don't care about food."

Sarah, pulse at her neck pounding wildly, sat back and pulled him toward her. "Anticipation makes everything better."

Sarah entered the restaurant, brushing Franco's arm as he held the door open for her. There was no way she was going to get through this lunch without touching him. Kissing him. If there was a dark booth in the back, she might even do something more wild.

Putting her hand on his chest, she blinked against the dim interior.

He covered her hand, lowering her fingers down his belly. She pulled back when she hit his belt buckle. His low chuckle washed over her like whiskey, invigorating her senses while bathing her in sensual warmth.

A woman came from the back, flour in her hair. Or maybe it was just gray? "Welcome! Oh, hello there," she said in friendly tones. "I remember you. Franco, right? I sent you home with an order of garlic knots."

He laughed and held out his hand. "That's me. They were delicious. I've brought...someone special...with me for lunch today."

Sarah also shook the woman's hand. "Pleased to meet you." The woman didn't sound at all Italian, and she looked nothing like what Sarah pictured someone might if they were from the swamps.

"I'm Lana. This way," the woman said, grabbing two plastic menus from the desk. She led the way to a side area where two other couples were already eating lunch. Four tables remained empty. "It's early still, but I've got a kitchen full of goodies."

"Thank you," Franco said, holding Sarah's chair for her.

Sarah murmured thank you, and watched him take his seat.

"Wine?" Lana asked, handing them each a menu.

"Sarah?" Franco asked.

She shook her head. "Iced tea. Unsweetened, please. With lemon."

"Two of those."

The woman nodded. "Coming up. Rolls? The lunch specials are in the middle. I'll be right back. I've been working on my chicken cacciatore."

"Is that what I smell? Porcini mushrooms?"

The woman laughed, pressing her hands to her belly. "Yes, yes. What else?"

"Rosemary." Franco sniffed the air. "White wine, tomatoes."

"You are good, sir."

"I'll have that, please."

"You don't want to read the menu?" Lana's smile creased her face and her eyes shone.

"No. I want your specialty. What else do you have back there?"

"Lasagna with veal sausage."

"I'll have an order of that as well."

Sarah handed her menu back. "I'll have what he's having." Yes, she was independent, but she could follow when it was a good idea.

"Your gentleman knows delicious food," the older woman said with an acknowledging nod.

"Yes, he does." And how to kiss, and touch, and enjoy life to the fullest. Heaven help her, but her mother's warning about being in over her head didn't even matter. Her heart was already in the deep end.

Franco covered her hand, his strength enveloping her. "We will try one of everything." His thumb brushed over her knuckles as he and the woman picked a feast.

Sarah didn't care what they ate, so long as she was here, with Franco.

Was it wrong?

A hook up would be impossible, because her feelings were involved. A love affair would hurt nobody but herself, so long as they kept it from Bella. The chance to be with Franco, even if just for a few hours, didn't hurt anybody. She wouldn't create expectations, she would be in the present.

The decision made, Sarah let herself be open to him, scooting closer as the garlic knots arrived.

"It's a good thing we are both eating these," she said. "I plan on kissing the hell out of you after lunch. I'd hate to kill you with my breath."

Franco stopped mid-bite, his eyes darkening with desire. "You do?"

She nodded, wishing they could skip lunch and go back to her apartment.

"I wish I hadn't ordered so much," he said. "Do you think we can get it to go?"

Laughing, she put her hand on his knee beneath the table.

Her phone dinged and she pulled away from Franco, getting her phone from her purse. Two texts from her mother. One wanting to know how things were going, the other letting her know that there was a call about a cat in a pool, but Martin was handling it. To take the day off.

A missed call came from Courtney, but no message. *Not good.* She'd specifically asked for an extension, and if the answer was yes, Courtney would have said so. No message meant no extension, and her friend would want to break it to her gently.

"Are things all right?" Franco asked, wiping a drop of butter from his full lower lip.

She swallowed and dropped the phone back into her purse. She wouldn't let the news ruin her day. "Yeah. Martin has to fish a cat from a pool. He doesn't like the water."

"The cat?"

"No, Martin." She let her eyes crinkle but didn't smile.

His lips curled upward. "Does that happen a lot?"

"More than you would think. Cat's get curious about floating things and that sometimes gets them in trouble." *Like me, curious about Franco.*

"They can swim?"

"Sure, but they don't like it. And they can't get out, usually."

"Martin can handle this. How often do you take a day off?" He leaned on one elbow, his hair falling forward over his forehead. He focused on her, and she basked in the attention.

"I've only been in business a year. I need to be there." She liked to think she was needed, anyway.

"How about you take a break? Fly with me somewhere?" He reached across the table for her hand. "I'm serious this time. We can be in Costa Rica tonight."

Sarah sat back in her chair, the wooden slats poking into her spine, both hands in her lap. He lived a completely different life. "Don't be ridiculous." She frowned, studying his expression. "I'm not free, and neither are you. Bella?"

"Bella has vacations. Weekends off." Now it was his turn to frown. "I see what you mean."

Sarah pointed between them. "We should just have lunch, and get back to our normal lives. Forget about kissing." And other amazing things she could only imagine. If his kisses were enough to make her head spin, how would he be in her bed?

He drank half of his tea in one go, setting the red

plastic glass on a napkin. "I don't want to forget about it."

Lana came out, followed by a waiter carrying six different plates. "I am so happy that you came today," she said. "I made you smaller plates of our best dishes, so you can taste it all."

Sarah stifled her frustration behind the napkin she held to her lips. She saw the tick at Franco's jaw before he smiled with thanks toward Lana. "It smells divine. I think I'll have that glass of wine now."

Holding one finger up in the air, Sarah nodded. "I'll take one too." Maybe a bottle to share was in order. Being tempted with desire, thwarted by pasta and tomato sauce, was too much to handle sober.

Steaming dishes were uncovered, revealing more food than she'd seen in months. "Mussels?" She looked at each platter in amazement. Who went into a restaurant and ordered everything on the damn menu? A man used to getting what he wanted. "Scallops? Chicken, fish, lasagna. What is that in front of you, Franco?"

"This is the cacciatore." He breathed in the steam and closed his eyes. "You will love this, Sarah. Just wait and see." He winked at her and she knew he was talking about more than the feast in front of them. "Trust me. I know what I'm doing."

Chapter Sixteen

Sarah put her hand on the passenger door of the Ferrari as Franco pulled into her driveway. The interior of the car smelled like garlic, but not even that could put a dent in the sexual tension she'd tried so hard to ignore on the drive home. Franco had kept his hand on the back of her neck, lightly tracing the delicate bones with his thumb and fingers. His touch made her entire body stand on point. *Electric.* Would they make love? Wouldn't they? They didn't speak, as if that might break the spell.

"Would you like to come in?" She didn't recognize

the deep tones of her voice.

He removed his hand and she wanted to cry at the loss. Franco gestured to the time blinking on the dash. "I have an hour before I need to pick Bella up from school." He eyed her, his hands twisting on the steering wheel, his jaw tight. "I know what I want to do. What do you want?"

Sarah wet her lips, every inch of her aware of Franco. Craving Franco despite the heavy meal in her belly. Despite knowing she was out of her league. If she sent him away, she might never know the feel of him again. They were playing with fire, and she *would* get burned. But for once, she didn't care.

She unbuckled her seatbelt. Martin had said he'd bring her the truck when he closed up for the afternoon. Hours from now. Her dogs were at the warehouse with her mom.

Was she tempting fate?

Or torturing herself with what could never be hers for more than a few stolen hours at a time?

Just one time, she told herself, leaning across the console to kiss him. Then later they could see what the future might hold. No expectations. "I want you."

After a light brush of her mouth across his, he nodded and turned off the car. "I should probably see you inside. As a gentleman."

He met her gaze. Held it.

She didn't want him to be a gentleman, but she sure did want him to come inside.

She swallowed and waited for him to come around to her side of the car. They were going to do it. *Make love.* Her breath seemed caught in her chest, her heart pounding so hard surely he could hear it.

Opening the door of the car, he reached down for her hand and lifted her up. His touch made her stomach tighten with anticipation. Need. Her blood was on fire causing goose bumps to prickle her skin. Just the idea of Franco in her house, in her bedroom, in her bed, made her mouth dry.

She moistened her lips, almost tripping over her own sandals as he touched the small of her back. Lifted the silky fabric to caress the bare skin at her spine.

"Your keys?" he asked, voice unrecognizable and deep.

Sarah pulled them from her purse, leading the way to her front door as if they'd had a bottle of wine instead of just one glass each. "Here."

He stayed at her back as if glued to her, his hands on her hips. She felt his arousal and it heightened her own. He stood behind her, breaths coming warm against the side of her face. He bent down and licked her ear, making her hot and cold at the same time.

"Are you sure?" he rumbled.

She opened the door, wanting him so badly it hurt. She yanked him inside and pushed the door closed, locking it behind them. "This way." Hand in hand, she led him through her foyer. She heard her breaths, heard his, too. Passion was a tangible thing, something she tasted in the air around them. Felt in the electricity between them.

They got five steps down the hall before he turned and pinned her against the wall. "I need you." He crushed her mouth to his in a searing kiss, teasing the seam of her mouth with his tongue. "Let me in."

Nodding, she molded against him as he ran his hands from her shoulders, down her arms to her waist, her hips, her stomach. He lifted her shirt and pulled it over her head, dropping kisses along her collarbone as he pulled her close.

The rigid length of him pressed against her hip and her core ached with need. It had been so long...if she was honest, hell, she'd never felt like this before. As if she would *die* if she didn't have sex with Franco de Silva, right now.

She buried her hands in his hair as he kissed her breasts. He teased her nipples through the thin fabric of her bra.

Tugging him down the hall, they went another few steps before Franco gathered her in his arms and lifted her up. She wrapped her legs around his waist, and he lowered her so that she rode him as he walked. Arching against him brought pleasure so intense her eyes watered and her breasts tightened.

He groaned. "Your bedroom?"

She pressed against him, not letting go. "Last door." Sarah leaned into his chest and kissed him hard. "On the left."

He moved slowly, his hands on her hips, her ass, her waist, in her hair and along her spine until they finally reached her bedroom.

She didn't care that the bed wasn't made. All she wanted was Franco.

Primal.

He dropped her on the bed, unbuckling his belt as she sprawled backward, trying to catch her breath.

Franco was beautiful in a classic way. Dark curls, heavy brows, lush lower lip and stubble along his jaw. Realizing that she liked watching him undress, he slowed his pace as he drew his shirt off, revealing a firm set of abs and a pleasure line from his navel into his jeans. Rose-colored nipples beaded beneath her stare.

"You're gorgeous," she said, not recognizing her own voice.

"I am glad you like what you see." He leaned over her, tracing the outline of her cheekbones with a tender caress. "I know we will be magical together."

His Brazilian male arrogance seemed perfect for the bedroom. For once she didn't want to set him straight.

"I will make you soar, *querida*."

She tugged at him, hoping to topple him onto the bed, but he stepped away to unbutton his jeans and slide them down past his hips.

He kicked them off and stood before her in black boxer briefs that left nothing to her imagination.

Golden skin, dark hair, a stiff erection all made her feel as if she was way too hot to be wearing any of her clothes.

Intuitive in a lover's way, he knelt at her side and slid her bra off. Her breasts, free, pebbled beneath his gaze. She leaned into him as he brushed his thumbs over her nipples.

"Let me," he said, gently pushing her backward.

She was putty. A knot of erogenous zones begging to be touched.

He gave her a sensual half-smile that promised much. Sliding her shorts down, he kept her panties in place, tossing her clothes to join his jeans.

She laid back, her skin damp. Franco brought her wrists over her head, holding her with one hand and caressing her trembling flesh with the other.

"You are beautiful." He released her wrists, wrapping her hair around his fingers and pulling her upward for a kiss. "Your eyes hold secrets, Sarah. A mystery I want to unfold."

"No mystery," she said in a low voice, unable to keep from touching him. His waist, his belly, his shoulders, his ass. The teasing sweep of his erection against her made her want to cry. "An open book."

Franco leaned down on one side, sliding his knee over her thigh. Pinning her, so he could trace the outline of her ribs. The concave of her lower belly. The lace of her panties. When she tried to rise, to move, he kept her still with one hand on her hip. "No woman is easy to read. You captivate me."

He brought his hand up the swell of her breast and she groaned. "Hurry, Franco." She turned her body toward his, skimming her hand over the musculature of his ass, the stiffness of him, straining against the cotton of his briefs. "I want you inside me."

"Americans. Always in such a rush," he whispered, teasing her with light kisses along her throat. He inched his hand, his fingers, lower. Lower. Hovering over her before gently pressing down against her.

She moaned and lifted her hips, overcome with desire.

"All right, my love." He slid her panties down, throwing them to the side, and let her help free himself of his briefs. The golden length of him left her speechless and she reverently caressed his shaft, rubbing her thumb over the tip. Back and forth, getting to know the velvety feel of his flesh in her palm. His breath hitched, his eyes half-closed in pleasure.

"Enough," he growled, pressing her back against the bed, his hand on her hip, then in one swift motion, his cock between her legs.

Sarah cried out, flooded by sensation. Franco filled her, touched her, invaded her. Wave of pleasure from the inside out made her quiver. And yet she craved more of him. No, not more, all—she wanted *all* of Franco.

He pumped deeply into her, his motions controlled

to keep her coming, to lengthen her pleasure. He leaned on one elbow, his hand buried in her hair as he continued. Stroke. Stroke. "You are so beautiful, Sarah."

She lifted her hips in rhythm with his. He made her feel like a goddess. One of the sexy ones with all of the power. She kept her eyes closed, swept away by his skill as a lover. The raging fire they built together.

Unbelievable, that she was rising again. The pinion of his hips bringing her higher. Higher still.

One, two three.

Sarah cried out in ecstasy, opening her eyes to memorize the look on Franco's face, the intensity of his coming as he ground into her welcoming body.

He held her close as they came down in a slow spiral.

Franco, his hand still tangled in her hair, dropped his forehead forward on the pillow, nestled next to her shoulder.

"Thank you," Sarah said, her heart racing as she ran her finger down his strong back. He lay on his stomach, half on her, half on the mattress.

"For what?" he mumbled.

"For showing me what they're always talking about in Cosmo. I've never had fireworks before." She kissed his jaw, his mouth. "Not like that."

Franco lifted himself up, his hand still caught in her hair, as if it anchored him to her and he didn't want to let go. "What you and I just felt cannot be found in Cosmo."

She looked like a siren, corn silk hair spread out on the pillow, her eyes at half-mast, dilated with pleasure. With the secret knowledge that made women sexy as hell. Sarah amplified the look, secure and confident in her ability to please.

As she laughed at him, caressing him, Franco fell for her, hard. His heart opened wide, realizing she was genuine. Sincere.

There were no games with Sarah. Just give and take, as equals. She claimed they were in different leagues but he didn't see that. True, he had more money. What was money but a means to an end?

Franco pulled his hand free of Sarah's hair, slowly, memorizing the texture. The scent of coconut shampoo. He only had one complication in a relationship with Sarah, and that was his daughter.

He would never put Bella in harm's way. But Bella saw the goodness in Sarah, too. Probably before he did, since he'd been so angry about the citation. But now? Franco admitted to himself that while he'd been hesitant over opening his heart, it was too late. Sarah was already inside. In his mind, he imagined them together. A perfect fit.

Sitting up, he pulled her with him so they were face to face. He leaned over and kissed her, just because he could, the velvety texture of her mouth addicting. "We should go slow." If he had his way, Sarah would move up to the Penthouse this afternoon. For Bella's sake, to let her get used to the idea, they would go out on dates. Separate, but also as a trio.

Sarah blinked, the confidence in her gaze vanishing. "Slow?" She backed up until she hit the bamboo headboard. "I never said I wanted a relationship with you, Franco."

Hurt, he narrowed his eyes. "What?"

"We can stay friends." Her voice was brittle.

His gut clenched and he reached for the sheet. Always this talk about being friends. "With benefits?"he ground out. Had she just used him?

Sarah flushed. Because she was naked, he saw that the rose color started between her breasts and moved upward to her cheeks. "Maybe we shouldn't do this again," she whispered.

"Let me understand you. We had an amazing, explosive encounter and yet you do not want to make love again?"

"I do want to," she said, her hair soft around her angry face. "But I can't. I thought I could handle you, and me, without..." She cleared her throat and patted her chest. "Taking it slow?" Sarah blinked quickly.

"I just meant," he said, wanting to explain. Realizing he'd hurt her. He wanted Sarah in his life, but he was a package deal.

She interrupted him, pulling the comforter up to her

breasts. "People in my world don't just hop on a plane to go check out a restaurant. We don't decide to buy an entire litter of puppies because we don't know which one we like the best. We don't order one of everything on the menu for lunch. We won't work out, you and I. You're smart to see it. I thought that maybe..."

"I said go slow, Sarah, not stop!" Franco lifted one finger, on the defense. How in the hell was this going so wrong?

She tightened her mouth and looked away.

"There are benefits to having money. Spending it on what I like is my prerogative. I refuse to apologize for that." What kind of woman didn't like nice things? Or want a man who could treat her like a queen? Sarah was different. Independent. Proud.

She would never abandon her family.

"You have Bella, and she is—as she should be—the light of your life. People have needs, and we satisfied those. That doesn't mean," Sarah faltered, making Franco wonder how much she believed the crap she was spouting, "That we need to have anything more than a friendship. I mean, I really appreciate your help with the dog treats."

"I haven't done anything." He felt cold, shut out. Mad. "You won't let me help you."

"You have helped, Franco."

"How?" He had the contacts to make her a household name if she would just swallow her pride.

"Your offer to carry them in your store?" Sarah

twisted her hair back over her shoulder, her gaze not fogged with lust now, but clear with determination. "Unless you've changed your mind?"

She thought he was the kind of guy to back out of an arrangement just because she wouldn't have a relationship with him? Angry, he said in harsh tones, "I understand that you need the roof, Sarah."

She winced, tucking the comforter tight around her body. "If I don't get that roof taken care of within the next two weeks, then I lose the warehouse. My Pet Rescue business. Everything that I've worked so hard for will be gone."

Was it an American thing to spend an afternoon with a lover, and then talk about business in bed? Franco didn't like it. And he could fix it. Why didn't she see that? He reached out and gently traced her arm with his finger.

"I want you in my life, Sarah. I will give you the money to repair your roof. So stop worrying, *querida.* It will be done tomorrow."

She sucked in a ragged breath. Her green eyes turned wide, and her face paled. "You can't buy me, Franco." She pulled away from him, scooting to the opposite edge of the bed.

What? He read the digital clock next to Sarah's bed. "Shit. I've got to go." Bella would be out of school in fifteen minutes. He hated leaving on such a note. "I'm already late." He saw that she was barely holding back tears, and assumed she was not pleased about his offer to pay for her roof.

"I'm sorry." He apologized, hoping that would give him time to fix this situation—later.

"Don't be." She swallowed and slid her gaze to the bedroom door. "Just, go."

He got out of the bed and slid his briefs and jeans on, picking up his shirt and clutching it in one fist so that he didn't actually punch something.

"Sarah." His heart ached, willing her to see how he really felt. Not the words that came out of his mouth, thoughtless words.

She stayed on the bed without saying anything refusing to even look at him.

"I'll call you later," he said.

"Don't."

Chapter Seventeen

Franco picked up Bella in the Ferrari, which was a treat since he normally drove her around in the Volvo, or what he thought of as the silver tank.

"Daddy!" Bella climbed in, worry on her face. "You were late."

"I'm sorry, honey." He leaned over and kissed her forehead. "I'm here now."

Switching moods, she said excitedly, "We get to drive the sports car. Did you like the puppies? Did you get a black one? Where is Sarah? What is that smell?

Pizza?"

Laughing eased his tension and he allowed his daughter's rambling to distract him from Sarah, and Sarah's rejection of anything besides friendship. He would not be friends with her. *Only* friends. He wanted more. He wanted it all. How to get past her pride?

"Sarah and I had Italian food for lunch." He waved at the principal and left the parking lot. "Take a big sniff. Know what it is?"

Bella inhaled deeply. "Garlic?"

"Good job." She was likely to have the discerning palate his mother handed down to him. "I have some leftovers that I think you might like."

"Where is Sarah?"

"She had work to do. She can't just play all the time with you." *Or me.*

"I hope you at least found a black puppy." Bella's lower lip jutted out.

"We did find one that we liked, but remember, they are for sale at the store."

"I know. I just get to pet them until they find their new home. Like Sarah's shelter."

God, was every conversation going to lead back to his elusive temptress? "Paisley will need to be walked as soon as we get home. Do you have homework?"

"I do. Spelling. But I got a hundred percent on my math test!"

"Well done, princess. That might deserve a small ice

cream cone. Or would you rather have a caramel apple?"

Bella rubbed her stomach. "Mmmm. I don't know yet what my stomach wants."

"All right." He tugged on one of her long, dark braids and pulled into the underground parking of their condo. "We can walk Paisley downtown and stop in at the store to tell Myra about the new puppies."

"Yes!" She shouted, pumping her small fist in the air. "New puppies."

They parked and Franco wondered if Sarah was right that they were better off ending an affair now. Adding her into his life would change things. Maybe Bella was better off getting his one on one attention. He'd never been late to pick up his daughter before.

He'd never left a woman in tears in bed before.

Uncertainty rattled him and he strode into the elevator, stepping back to let Bella push the button to go up. "When do we get to pick up the new puppy? I want to go. In the sports car, *vroom, vroom.*" She spun around inside the elevator like a brunette top.

"Next week. But we have to get the okay from Dr. Wilton first. Just to make sure." He'd been impressed with the Brownings set up and liked their policies regarding the puppies. They'd even passed Sarah's eagle eye, so he anticipated no problems from his own vet.

"Can we name her Blackie?"

"We are not keeping her, Bella. Paisley is enough."

"I know, Daddy," his daughter said, glancing at him

from the corner of her eye. She was plotting something, he was pretty sure.

They got off on their floor and Bella raced to the door. He unlocked it, and his daughter zoomed to Paisley's crate. Had he ever had so much energy?

Could be the wine, food and sex this afternoon had zapped his strength.

No regrets. But he could sure use a cup of coffee.

"Come on, Bella. Do you have Paisley's leash?"

Sarah searched for her phone as it rang, hoping it wasn't Franco. She'd hated that wounded look in his eyes as he'd apologized. Wanting to go slow, sure, maybe she could have gotten past his off-the-cuff remark. She understood he had a daughter, for heaven's sake.

But telling her not to worry, he wanted her in his life? For how long? A week? A month?

And don't worry, baby, I'm paying for your roof? Sarah scrubbed tears from her eyes.

I can't be bought.

It was painfully clear that they were worlds apart, despite the incredible pleasure they'd shared. Sniffling, she found her phone on the floor by the front door where it must have fallen when she'd dragged Franco inside.

She picked it up and saw Martin's smiling face. "Hey," she answered, trying for cheerful and hoping to hide her tears.

"What's wrong?" Martin asked, honing in on her mood. He was good that way.

"Nothing. How's it going? Did you get the cat out of the pool?"

"Of course." He snorted. "Can I drop the truck off? I still don't understand why Franco didn't bring you to the office."

"He was running late and I had a head ache." *I made a mistake.*

Martin paused, as if pondering her words and weighing them for truth.

"I can jog over, if it's out of the way," Sarah said to distract him. Another plus in the small town column was nothing was ever too far.

"It's hot as Hades, so don't you dare." He sighed. "I'll bring the fur-babies over too. It's been quiet, so your mom went home an hour ago."

"Thank you for taking on today for me."

"You should let me do it more often."

Why didn't she? Oh yeah. Money. If things were short, she ate peanut butter and crackers. She couldn't stiff her employee. "Thank you, Martin. As we get busier, you know that I will."*If the whole thing didn't come crashing around her.*

"Courtney called. About the fundraiser? She said we can do a carwash and barbecue in our parking lot. She asked that you call her, about the roof. I swear I didn't bring it up."

A bad feeling rumbled in her stomach. "All right. I'll do it now."

"See you soon." Martin hung up.

Sarah stared at the phone, knowing she had to call Courtney. Knowing it wouldn't be good news regarding the extension.

If she had the kind of money Franco tossed around on a whim, she wouldn't have any worries about keeping her business running. Getting a roof. Protecting the unwanted pets in the world. She shook her head, knowing she would rather fold Pet Rescue than take his cash. She would find another way.

If her life was centered around making money, she would've stayed in school to be a vet. Married. Sarah had chosen her path, and she just had to stick with it. Sometimes it was damn hard.

She dialed Courtney's number and let it ring.

"Hey!" Courtney said, out of breath. "I called you earlier."

"Yeah, I just spoke to Martin. He said something about the roof?"

There was a long moment where Sarah could hear her heart beat in her eardrums before Courtney said, "I talked to Randall Wallace. He told me that we have a PetGiant that wants to move in. Your warehouse is the perfect size."

A PetGiant? A big chain, in their little town by the

sea? "I thought that was against the community feel."

"They've agreed to follow the standard design, and blend in with the other buildings." She coughed and then cleared her throat. "It's a lot of money for the city."

"But the building is mine. My business provides a service."

"That's true. Sort of. The building was sold to you very inexpensively, with the caveat that you would get the roof fixed within six months. We extended that to one year, which is up in two weeks. The council can't extend it again. I'm sorry, Sarah. You know I voted against it."

Sarah bowed her head. Could today get any worse? "I'll figure it out."

"There is a lot of money at stake for the city," Courtney explained. "Randall is pressuring all of the businesses to up their bottom line."

Not one to stay down for long, Sarah's mind raced ahead. "I need to make this fundraiser rock."

"I'll help where I can."

"That won't piss off the powers that be?" Randall Wallace had inherited the town a while back, and wasn't as savvy a manager as his father had been. He didn't hold with the same vision, either, being more concerned with money.

"We are all about hometown community," Courtney said. "Just read the city brochure. I can't tell anybody about the proposed PetGiant, and neither can you. But I want you to get that new roof. Come on down and pick up the paperwork you need for the fundraiser. A car wash will rally the community."

"I'll be there in a few minutes."

Sarah hung up. She'd ridden an endorphin high, safe in Franco's arms. Now, she'd crashed and it took all she had to crawl into the shower.

Her sensitive skin was too tender, her heart bruised by what couldn't be. Ignoring feelings that left her vulnerable, Sarah focused on what she could physically change. Car wash? Yuck, but she'd spread the word and get donors for raffle prizes. Martin would have to run the barbecue. There was no way she would let Franco help her now. She didn't even want him to carry the treats in his store.

She would sell those dog treats door to door if she had to.

Dressing in black shorts and a fitted t-shirt, Sarah was ready to go by the time Martin arrived.

She gave the dogs bacon treats, pet them, and turned to Martin. "Want some water or iced tea?"

"No, ma'am." He scrutinized her from head to toe. "There is something different about you," he said, tapping his lower lip.

"My hair is down," Sarah said, trying to throw him off track. "I talked to Courtney. We're going to need every woman we know who looks good in a bikini to come help at the car wash. Next Saturday. If we don't get the money, I lose my business." Sarah blinked before she cried. No crying. *Just do it.*

"That seems harsh." Martin crossed his arms.

"I guess there's some paperwork I have to sign, so I'm going to do that now. Courtney said she'd do her best to get word out, too. But I'm thinking we need flyers and a radio ad, anything to get people to spend their money with us next weekend."

"Got it. The jars will be here tomorrow for the treats. Your mom and I were talking, and what do you think about a hand-painted stencil for the Happy Treats?"

Sarah nodded. "Sounds great. We can paint at the office."

"Different colors for different flavors? Keep it visual."

"Thank you, Martin. Yes. I like it." She pressed her hand to her stomach, nervous because so much relied on selling a product she hadn't even baked yet.

He came around the counter in her kitchen and gave her a hug. "You can do this. We can help."

"I count on you more than you realize, Martin."

"What are friends for? Do you mind dropping me back at the office, so I can get my car?"

"No problem."

Thirty minutes later, Sarah arrived at Courtney's office. "All right, Courtney. Where do I sign?"

Courtney got up from behind her desk. In slacks and a floral blouse, she was the epitome of professional. "Here. Listen, I made up some flyers, just simple ones, but

I thought you could pass them out downtown? I'll hang one up in the foyer and have a stack on the counter."

Sarah's eyes welled. She and Courtney had been friends since grade school. They knew this town, they knew the community. "I should have started this sooner. We've been busy, though, and I just thought the money would come in faster. But every time it came in, it went out—somewhere else." *I really wanted to do it myself.*

Courtney put her hand on Sarah's shoulder and squeezed. "I understand. Businesses take time to get up and running. I don't want you to go anywhere." She handed over a stack of flyers. "The city will put together a gift basket. Make sure you get donations, okay? Now go! We only have a week to pull this off. I know you wanted a formal dinner but talk about impossible. Next time, don't wait so long to ask for help, all right?"

Her independence was kicking her in the ass.

Sarah started at the pier and worked her way up Commercial Boulevard, saying hello to old friends as well as new ones. She stopped at Ambrosia and ordered a pecan nutty bun and a mango iced tea. So far, everybody she'd talked to had been happy to donate.

"How's business, Celia?"

Celia Langford was relatively new to the area and, like Sarah, had opened her own business. Organic food and delicious teas instead of unwanted pets, but still, the bottom line was the bottom line.

A cool blonde, Celia slid a napkin across the counter

and smiled. “Good. I love it here.” There’d been an issue with the town’s owner, Randall Wallace, but she’d prevailed. Sarah admired her resilience a great deal and hoped to follow suit.

“How’s Dax?”

Celia and Dax Smith, owner of the local dive shop, had fallen head over heels for one another. Love at first bite. Sarah had known Dax and his family all her life and was glad to see him happy.

“He’s getting better. It was tough for a while, with his dad dying.”

“Dave was a good guy,” Sarah said. “I saw Darcy hanging out at the beach. Is she sticking around?”

Celia shrugged, her eyes warming with concern. “I don’t know. She’s taking it really hard.”

“If there is anything I can do, just let me know.” She sipped the refreshing fruity tea and looked around the shop. Customers filled the tables both inside and out.

“Thanks. I’ll be sure to pass the message along.”

“So, how would you like to donate to my upcoming fundraiser? Or better yet, get into a bikini and wash some cars? You’d stop traffic.”

“Causing an accident is not my idea of a good time,” Celia laughed, poking fun at herself as she patted her hips. “But I will gladly donate a few meals for the cause. What cause are we talking about?”

“I need a new roof.”

“Ah.”

"Within the next two weeks. The fundraiser will be Saturday. Tell everybody you know, okay?"

Celia blew out a breath, her eyes wide. "That is cutting it close."

"I know." Sarah finished the last of her nutty bun. "I'm working on my time management skills."

Laughing, Celia took her empty dish and tapped the counter. "Good luck."

Next, Sarah went down the opposite side of the street, starting with the Greek restaurant. Before she realized it, she stood in front of the pet store.

Puppies dozed in the window front, each cubicle clean with a water bottle and a toy or blanket. A white and tan Shitzu blinked, shiny black eyes rolling back in its head as it went back to sleep. In the next cubicle was a Beagle mix, with long ears and brindle coloring. Adorable.

Should she go inside? She didn't want Franco's help, but she needed that new roof. They'd made love and that changed everything.

Pride is an ugly thing, Sarah, she told herself as she walked by the front door without going inside.

"Sarah!"

She immediately recognized Bella's joyful voice and turned to look in the shop. Bella stood next to a plump woman with glasses and a smile that slipped as she recognized Sarah without the Pet Rescue uniform.

"Hi, Bella."

The little girl skipped to the sidewalk. "I'll be right here, Myra," Bella called out, taking Sarah's free hand. "What do you have, Sarah?"

"Just some flyers."

"What for?"

"The fundraiser for Pet Rescue."

"I want to come. Isn't Daddy going to cook?"

No. She couldn't be around Franco and focus on what needed to be done for her business. "I don't think so. But you are certainly welcome to come and get your car washed."

The enormity of what she needed to put together made her stumble and she quickly balanced herself against the building.

"Are you all right, Sarah?"

Looking up, she saw that Franco's eyes were filled with concern. His husky tones sent shivers down her spine, in a way her body remembered well. She pulled away. It was fitting that he see her hot, flushed and overwhelmed. She was never at her best around him. "I'm fine."

"Can I get you a bottle of water? Come inside, where it's air conditioned. What are you passing out?"

He pulled her into the shop, her skin tingling where his fingers held hers. Glitter and glitz made her blink against the bling. Designer poochie carriers to rhinestone studded strollers, Franco had something for everybody.

He wasn't acting any differently toward her. She

needed to buck up and do the same. "You've added to the inventory since I was in last."

Myra glared at her from the cash register. "We had just opened up, if I recall. When you gifted us with that stupid citation."

Franco rested his hand against her lower back and cleared his throat. "We've moved on since then, Myra. And we no longer use cleaning products that might be harmful to the puppies, so everything worked out well."

"Daddy, Sarah's going to have a car wash."

He scanned the flyer over her shoulder, then looked at her. "I'd be happy to cook. Whatever you need, Sarah."

Her tongue was tied. Franco took the flyers from Sarah's nerveless fingers. It was awful, terrible, that she wanted him. He was a dad, a business owner. An arrogant (but not really) Brazilian male. Rich. Gorgeous. Yes, arrogant, thinking he could buy happiness. *My happiness.*

Sarah crossed her arms at her waist. "If you could pass them out, I'd appreciate it. Martin is doing the barbecue. We're talking hamburgers and hotdogs, not crab cakes with sauce."

He frowned. "I don't mind."

"Martin will do it."

Franco's gaze cooled and he gave her a single nod. His touch left her back.

She swallowed, sick to her stomach. She felt as if she was breaking something tenuous, which was ridiculous. They barely knew each other. But that wasn't true, especially after today. They'd shared a magical day. This was reality.

He walked away from her and pointed to a partially empty shelf. "We're waiting for your dog treats. We've got space as soon as you've got them ready."

"You didn't mention that *she* made them," Myra said, taking off her glasses so she could glare at Sarah without anything in the way.

This time Franco didn't come to her defense.

"Thank you." She turned her back on his angry employee. "I appreciate that." She had to sell enough to save her roof. Business. Practicality. No emotion. She exhaled.

"Since you don't need me to cook, how else can I help? We would like to support our community." Franco tucked his hands into the front pockets of his jeans. "Right, Bella?"

Bella nodded, looking from Sarah to her dad as if sensing something wrong.

Sarah gritted her teeth. "Perhaps you'd like to donate something for our raffle?" If he said the roof, she'd scream.

"Definitely." Franco stared at her, his expression unreadable. "A chi-poo puppy."

"That's too much." She bit the inside of her cheek, feeling betrayed and confused. She hadn't realized how bitter regret would taste.

"I want to. I told you." He lowered his voice and

held her eyes. "My money, my prerogative on how I spend it."

"Right. Money buys everything."

This was so not the place for this, yet she couldn't help it.

Sarah's vision blurred. "But not me."

Franco winced.

She waved to Bella, called good-bye to Myra who obviously hated her, and left before she burst into tears.

Chapter Eighteen

Franco watched Sarah leave, her anger transcending any language barrier. Myra left her spot by the register and stood next to him.

"I think I've missed something?" she asked, her tone accusing. "Sleeping with the enemy?"

Franco sent his employee a warning look. "Myra." He put his hand on Bella's head. "Princess, will you see if you can find the box of dog brushes in the back?"

"Okay, Daddy!"

His daughter ran to the store room and Franco took

Myra's arm. "Listen. Sarah is not a bad woman. She is passionate about stopping illegal breeding practices. She stopped the mill operating out of this shop right before I bought it, and I can't blame her for being vigilant. Her heart is in the right place."

Myra scowled. "You like her. No, you *really* like her? Franco, be careful. She wanted to shut you down."

"That was before..." He cleared his throat.

Myra's eyes widened. "No. Tell me you didn't actually *sleep* with the enemy?"

"She's not the enemy!" Franco checked to make sure Bella was still in the back. "I care about her, Myra. But she won't give me a chance."

"Why?" Myra's shoulders stiffened. "She's an idiot. You're terrific."

"Thanks." He shifted uncomfortably. "So, you heard her talk about the fundraiser she's doing this weekend? It is for a new roof. Well, all I did was offer to pay for the roof being repaired, and she got very angry."

Myra's shoulders lowered and she sucked in her bottom lip. "Before or after, you know, you did the wild thing?"

"After." He shrugged.

She looked him square in the face. "How soon after?"

"Right after. I didn't realize how bad she needed it before, or I would have offered earlier!" Not that she would have accepted his help then, either. He bent his head toward Myra. "She had a problem, I gave her a solution. I don't understand what went wrong."

Myra sighed and shook her head. "You are such a man."

"Yes, I am." He crossed his arms over his slightly puffed out chest.

"Franco. I don't know her—"

"Sarah. Her name is Sarah."

"I don't know Sarah like you do, but I've seen enough of her to realize she's the kind of woman who wants to do things her way, by herself." Myra fiddled with the dog shampoos on the shelf. "Stubborn, one might say."

Franco nodded. "I like that she is independent. I want her to be independent with me. I can make her life better."

"Right," she said with a commiserating bob of her head. "But you can't say it like that to her without setting off all kinds of alarms. I heard her say that you couldn't buy her…"

His employee had excellent hearing if she got that over the barking puppies and influx of customers. "Sarah thinks that I use my money to get my way." He shrugged. "Money is a tool. Why not use it for what I want?"

Myra held up her hand. "Excellent point. However, when it comes to women, and things of an emotional nature, money needs to be off the table."

"I am not trying to buy her love. I offered to fix her

roof."

She slid her glasses back on her face. "Find out what is important to Sarah, besides the roof. Give her that."

Franco pulled at his chin. What made Sarah tick? "She has to help unwanted animals. She champions the underdog, literally."

"Why?"

He scowled, remembering the story Jennifer Murphy had shared with him. "Something happened when she was a little girl. She didn't get to save the dog."

Myra's attitude softened a hair. "So that scared her? Kids take that stuff to heart."

"She's spent her adulthood making up for what she views as a failure when she was just a child." Franco wondered if perhaps Sarah felt let down by the people in her life, and if that why she was so independent. "She takes care of things. By herself. But she doesn't have to be alone. I want to be with her."

Myra pointed at him with a red dog collar. "So you need to convince her that you are the type of man that can be a partner. Make her see that there is room for someone to stand at her side."

Bella ran out of the store room with an armful of dog brushes. "I found them, Daddy. Where do you want me to put them?"

Franco breathed out his frustration. "Bottom shelf, please. Thank you."

How to get Sarah to see his heart? "Excellent advice,

Myra." He snapped his fingers and scowled.

She grinned. "I never said it would be easy."

Franco didn't call.

She didn't call him, either.

Her days were crazy busy, but the first two nights were hell as she dissected every last nuance of their time together. I'm a grown woman, she told herself after another tear-soaked pillow and sleepless night, and I do not need anybody.

She'd replayed those last moments in her bed before he left, wishing things could have ended differently. Maybe she'd misunderstood when he said he'd wanted to take things slow, otherwise, why would he have looked hurt?

She'd tried to give him an easy way out. Offering to be just friends, and yet that seemed to piss him off.

Which had led to his telling her that he'd pay for her roof. *Not to worry*. He'd take care of it. I want you in my life. I'll take care of it tomorrow.

Grr! *Arrogant.*

Paying for the roof, paying her off. Her stomach churned. She wasn't a whore, to be bought and paid for.

She hoped deep inside he hadn't meant it like that. What did she want from him? If he called her, and she answered, what would they say? It was safer to hide behind anger and hurt than step outside her comfort zone.

She went into the office Wednesday morning pleased to see the jars of treats stacked for display on the shelf by the front door. "Morning, Martin," she called, waving at him in the kitchen by the coffee pot. "These turned out great."

"The stencil was the perfect idea. Want a cup?"

"Sure." Sarah eyed the jars critically. HAPPY TREATS stenciled in different colors along the side for different flavors of treats. Simple, but classic. "They don't look cheap," she muttered to the dogs at her feet.

Nashville meowed from the top of a stack of boxes by the front door. "What are these?" she asked, heading toward the smell of sanity in a mug.

"We already have an order for a hundred."

"Who?" Sarah asked, hope soaring.

"de Silva's Diamond Dogs."

Hope crashed. Was she making a mistake? Did he think she couldn't do this without his help? *What if I can't?*

"I told Franco I'd drop them off." Martin handed her a mug. "Since I wasn't sure you wanted him here. Not that you've said anything," he paused dramatically. "One way or the other."

They hadn't forced the issue. Tuesday morning, her mother asked about how the drive out west went and Sarah had burst into tears.

"I still don't want to talk about it." She brought the

coffee to her nose and sniffed. "Thank you, for offering to deliver them." She buried her confusion over her feelings for Franco in work, heading toward the desk and the computer. "I talked to a few of the boutique stores downtown and they want a couple dozen boxes each. Geez, only 1350 left to go."

She blinked quickly and took a big sip of coffee. *So much.*

"Honey, I understand about heart break, but things were going so well. Dinner, snorkeling, driving out to look at the puppies..."

"There wasn't ever a 'thing' between us. We are, were, just friends." Sarah kept her line of defense high. Denial worked.

"Baloney. I saw you after he cooked you dinner. Sparks!"

"Attraction between two people doesn't a relationship make," Sarah drawled. "I'm busy, Martin. I've got to save this business, or we are all out on our asses. Including the new batch of kittens that came in yesterday. I don't have time for day dreams."

"Sarah, you have not asked my opinion, but I am going to tell you this for your own good. Life is too short, too precious, to hide behind doing good works."

She whirled the office chair around and faced Martin. "Excuse me?"

He walked toward her, empathy in his eyes. "You are an amazing person. You have a huge heart." He put his hand on her arm. "I'm your friend. I admire everything that you are doing here. But I feel like you might be afraid to take a chance on love."

Stomach tight, Sarah tensed as if she were under attack. "You think I'm afraid?" Denial. Denial. "I didn't ask for your opinion. Why don't you take the truck and deliver those jars? I'll walk Buster this morning." How could he even suggest that she was hiding behind her business?

"I'm sorry, Sarah," Martin said, coming toward her with his arms outstretched for a hug.

Sarah, on the verge of losing her composure, and possibly the toast she'd had for breakfast, shook her head. "Go on."

He left without his hug and she ran her wrists under cool tap water in the kitchen to calm down. Benny and Pippa stared at her, as if sensing she was upset.

She sank down to the floor and the dogs scrambled into her lap as she cried. Damn it. She was not afraid of anything. How had Franco gotten into her heart so fast?

Chapter Nineteen

Fundraiser Day. She'd set the alarm early Saturday morning so that she got to Pet Rescue way before dawn. There was so much to do that she hadn't really slept well, anyway.

She opened the office door, her stomach tense. So much was riding on this. Martin had drawn a rocket on a piece of poster board with the number 1500 at the top, and colored in lines at the bottom as a visual toward their goal. They'd gone on the last few days as if he hadn't given his advice, as if she hadn't heard his words of concern. She was not afraid of love.

She bought him a barbecue apron in turquoise blue and a set of tongs to match. They had music planned from Martin's friend at the club who offered to DJ the event. Not in drag. She'd gotten ten extra hoses, clowns, balloons and three different face-painters.

Randall Wallace could just forget about PetGiant.

Her mom came in at seven, a box of donuts in hand. "I've got a good feeling about this," she said. "Nothing but clear skies predicted for today."

Buster barked in greeting, going over to nose the box. "No, no," her mom scolded and the big dog tucked his tail between his legs.

"Way to break his heart, Mom," Sarah said with a laugh. "He's such a baby."

"I would take him home, if I could. But Bert and Ernie are too old to share their spots on the couch."

"He's a good dog. We'll find Buster a place of his own." Sarah knew that in her bones. It was what she did best.

"You've sold 400 boxes of treats already?" Her mom set the donuts on the counter and came back to study the poster board. "That's terrific."

"Only 1100 to go." She rubbed the ache at her temples. "Do you still have my old Girl Scout uniform?"

"That's your plan? Door to door? Oh honey, you were never good at that." Her mom peeked back into the warehouse. "I love the lights! It's like a party."

"We've got the iguana, the bunny, Buster, and two batches of kittens. Oh, and Tom. But today isn't so much about finding them homes as it is showing the community what we do."

Her mom nodded and turned her eagle eye onto Sarah. "You look perfect."

White polo and khaki shorts. Sarah touched her pony tail. "Pretty basic. Just like me."

"There is nothing *basic* about you." Her mom wore jean shorts with fancy stitching along the back pockets and white polo that said Pet Rescue on the shoulder logo. "I was wondering if I should invite Leland," her mother said casually. "He might help at the cash register?"

"Who is Leland?"

"My...boyfriend." Her mom started laughing, her face flushed. "That sounds so funny."

"You went from dinner to boyfriend/girlfriend status already?" Sarah grinned.

"It's been a month since he first asked me out."

Sarah gave her mom a hug, refusing to think about Franco. "I'm so happy for you, really. And of course he can run the register. I'd appreciate all the help we can get."

Her phone dinged, signaling a text. She assumed it would be from Martin, but it was from Franco. She groaned and her mom asked, "What's wrong?"

"Uh." Sarah swallowed. "It's nothing."

"Nothing wouldn't make your cheeks pink. I'm sorry about Franco. Maybe he will show up today."

She hadn't shared much about what had happened, keeping the pain of it close to her heart. "He wants to come. I don't want him to."

"Why are you pushing him away?"

"Mom. He thinks he can solve everything with money."

"Yeah? So?"

"So." Flustered, Sarah shook her phone. "I can't be bought."

"Of course not. But accepting help is not a bad thing."

"Help? Help is not offering to pay for the roof." After sex. While they were still naked, in her bed. "That's taking over and trivializing how hard I've worked to make this business a success. Maybe not to his standards, but I've saved a lot of animals."

"He's not your ex." Her mom opened the box of donuts. "Franco wants to help because he cares about you. It's his way of showing it. It's a very Latino male thing."

"I don't like it."

"You'd rather lose the business?" She lifted a bear claw with white icing and took a bite.

"No! I'd rather find another way. Franco has to respect that I can do this on my own. I'm not like the rich and famous. I work to earn my way."

"That sounds an awful lot like pride talking."

Sarah stared at the phone in her palm, deciding not to answer Franco's text. She didn't want to be a fool, but she couldn't think about anything other than her roof at the moment. People and animals relied on her good sense. "You might be right, Mom. But unlike Franco, pride is all I have."

By ten in the morning, Sarah had a line of vehicles out to the street. The local high school had sent their cheer team to wash cars and generate enthusiasm with pom-poms and buckets of sudsy water.

Sarah had a video streaming non-stop in the office of Mrs. Drummel and other customers with their adopted pets. The police chief came by, as did the fire chief, all offering support. Nobody really liked Randall Wallace, and even though the PetGiant bid for her property was supposed to be a secret, it wasn't.

Courtney showed up with the Ft. Lauderdale news crew, giving Pet Rescue five minutes of precious air time. The jars of Happy Treats got a special mention, with her website and ordering information along the bottom of the screen.

Every time she heard a little girl's voice, she turned, hoping to see Bella. And yes, Franco. She missed him. Them. Her mother was right. She didn't like the way holding on to injured pride made her feel. Once this was over, no matter what the results of the day turned out to be, she would call Franco and apologize. No expectations after that.

By eleven, Sarah decided it was time to fire up the barbecue. Martin donned the turquoise blue apron and posed for a picture with her mother, who then introduced her to Leland.

Tall, with a head of shiny silver hair and a broad smile, Leland held out his hand. "Pleased to meet you, Sarah. Your mother raves about you, you know."

Sarah blushed. "Mom."

"What? I'm proud of you, for good reason. You've accomplished all of this," her mom waved to the full parking lot and the fair-like atmosphere of the fundraiser, "to follow your mission in life." Her mom stuck one hand on her denim-clad hip. "You'll just have to deal with it."

Sarah heard Franco's deep, rumbling laughter and her entire body lit up. "A parent's pride. Do you hear that Bella? You'll just have to deal with it, too."

Turning around, slowly, so she didn't give herself away, she faced Franco and Bella. Their matching smiles demanded one of her own, which she gave freely. "Hi! I am really glad you could make it."

Franco captured her gaze as if to call her out as a liar, but he didn't say a word. "It's all Bella has been talking about this morning. We are here to wash cars and help however we can."

"Thank God," Martin said, untying his apron and handing it over to Franco. "I so did not want to cook. I go out to eat." He shrugged and didn't look at Sarah.

"What do we have?" Franco walked over to the coolers and Sarah followed on his heels.

"Frozen meat," she said, hardly believing he was here. "Nothing special."

Franco looked at Bella, who had a cute purple backpack that she gave to her dad. "We brought a few spices," he said. "Just in case."

Sarah turned toward Martin, who pretended to study the clouds in the sky.

Bella laughed. "Daddy said I get to have my face painted like a cat."

Martin held out his hand for Bella. "I would be happy to escort you, young lady."

Franco nodded his approval, leaving Sarah wondering just what her friend had been up to behind her back. It didn't matter, though. She admitted to herself that she was glad Franco was here.

"I'm glad you came, Franco," her mom said. "I was hoping to get a taste of your culinary genius."

Leland chuckled. "Am I missing something?"

Sarah, feeling awful that Franco was being reduced to all-beef hot dogs on a gas grill, said, "He's a chef, actually. Talented. You won't be able to tell from this. Franco, I can do it. We can't have your reputation taking a hit when the product is inferior, compared to what you are used to."

"Sarah, I want to do this. Okay? Now, stand back and let me see what I've got to work with." He wore a white t-shirt and plaid shorts with black leather slides on his feet. He tied the apron on and then looked at her with a confidant wink.

She rolled her eyes but her heart sang. He was a beautiful man. "Veggie patties, beef patties. Hot dogs. With a side of chips or a scoop of potato salad. I'm your sous chef," she said with a self-deprecating laugh. "So don't expect too much."

"This ought to be good," her mom said, her eyes flashing with humor. "Leland and I will go get the salads from the kitchen."

Sarah gave Franco his space at the grill, watching as he seasoned the meat. "You look like you've done this before," she said. It was just the two of them and she wished she could touch him. Let him know that she was sorry.

"I like to grill." He looked at her, his face softening.

Her insides turned to mush and she stepped closer to him. "Thank you for coming today. I guess Martin talked you into it?"

His expression turned serious. "I wanted to help you in a way that would be acceptable to you. I'd rather cook than wash cars."

"I owe you an apology."

"Sarah, you don't." He didn't look at her as he got the cheese from the cooler. "Do you want to start separating the buns? We need to butter them up before we toast them."

"Sure." She untied the plastic bag of white hamburger buns and put on thin gloves. "Franco."

He turned toward her, leaning in so quick she didn't have time to pull away from the press of his mouth on hers. "Not now. Let's see how well we work together as a team. You'll see how much can be accomplished when you don't have to do everything yourself. A partner can be a very good thing."

Franco watched the sparkle in Sarah's eyes as she accepted his challenge. "Deal."

A lot was riding on his ability to run a gas grill and flip some burgers. But Franco was no stranger to pressure, and cooking was what he did best. "What are we selling these things for?"

Sarah, her hair back in a ponytail, her cheeks flushed with heat from the barbecue and the South Florida sun, attacked her sous chef duties with precision. Plastic gloves, a tray of buns, a butter knife and the tub of whipped butter. He watched, nodding with approval as she got all of the bread. "7 dollars for a burger, 8 for a cheeseburger, 5 for a hot dog."

"Reasonable."

"The stuff was donated from Publix."

"Smart girl. How is it you didn't have the money for the roof? You seem like you have a good understanding of business." He kept his tone conversational and hoped that he hadn't pissed her off again.

She sorted the paper plates and plastic utensils. "I had half of the money, but then the air conditioner went out. I can't have a warehouse without air conditioning for the animals. I'm supposed to be saving them, not suffocating them."

Franco put the first row of burgers down on the heated rack. The sizzle reminded him of other fun times. Sure, maybe there were sirloin burgers and champagne instead of frozen patties but he wouldn't trade a second of that for where he was right now.

"You did what you had to do."

She gave him a grateful smile. "Thanks, Franco."

"So, I heard a rumor that PetGiant wants to buy your warehouse."

"Where did you hear that? Courtney swore me to secrecy, but you're the third person to bring it up."

How totally Sarah to honor a secret, no matter how awful the consequences. "The fire chief. We became friendly after meeting at Bella's school a few weeks ago. Nice guy."

Garlic and onion powder wafted through the air on the steam from the grill and he noticed that people were starting to gather.

"I've got five hundred boxes of treats sold. I need to sell a thousand more and I'll have enough money for the roof."

"I love the stencils. And the customers are giving really great feedback on them, which is a big deal for return business."

"Thank you, for your help. I mean, it was your idea to add the honey and cut the rye with the wheat flour. Carrying them in your shop."

He flipped the burgers and gestured for her to set the buttered buns on the toasting rack. They worked together as if they'd done it forever. He was tempted to kiss the back of her neck when she reached across him for the top rack.

Instead, he stole a sniff of her coconut shampoo.

"It was my pleasure."

"Franco de Silva! There you are."

Franco looked up with a smile. He watched Sarah look up too.

"I never thought I'd see you in a blue apron. Have times gotten that tough?"

Chapter Twenty

Sarah lifted her chin, ready to do battle. "This is a fundraising event, sir. Mr. de Silva is here as a volunteer."

The red-haired man laughed, not at all offended. "Mr. de Silva. You've got this sweet thing fooled."

Bristling, Sarah glanced at Franco to see how he knew this joker.

Instead of being upset, Franco came around the grill to give the man a hug. "Charlie Beckett. Meet Sarah Murphy."

He held out his hand and she noticed his brilliant blue

eyes and pale skin that somehow didn't clash with his cherry-red hair. "Sarah, am I thrilled to meet you. Has Franco told you about me?"

"No," she said, shaking her head.

"My job is to find the best new thing and market the hell out of it. I make money, the customer makes money. It's a win-win. Franco, you don't want those burgers to burn, do you?"

Franco hustled back behind the grill. "Charlie's a slick-talker, Sarah, so don't sign on the bottom line until you have a lawyer look it over."

Charlie stuck his hands over his heart. "Ouch." He looked at Sarah and grinned. "I hired Franco for special events. Amazing chef. He's got a gifted palate. And he's not cheap either. How'd you get him?"

"He is supporting his community. Why are you here?" she asked, nerves tingling her spine.

"The dogs love your Berrylicious Biscuit.I think we can make some money together." He took her to the side. "People want to know what their pets are eating is good for them. The best. I know I do."

Sarah turned to Franco, who was engrossed in cooking burgers. She quickly ran back behind the grill to save the toasted buns from being burned. She piled everything on a tray and started to laugh. "Really, Franco? I don't think you can help but be a hero. Swooping in to save the damsel in distress."

"You don't need saving, Sarah. I invited him to try

it, that's all. It was your final product that got him interested."

Cooking kept her from really accepting the possible good news. She looked up as her mom and Leland came out of the office.

Sarah shook her head. "It shouldn't have taken that long to get the potato salad."

"Leland seems like a good guy," Franco said. "Everybody deserves somebody."

Charlie peered over the grill. "I deserve a cheeseburger."

"We're almost ready," Sarah said, bustling around the small area. "That will be eight bucks."

He pulled out his wallet. "What are we fundraising for?"

"A new roof." Sarah pointed to the warehouse and the "ugly" patch.

Charlie looked at her and grinned from Franco back to her. "Sarah, with your Happy Treats marketed by me, you can have ten roofs."

Her mom came up just in time to hear the last part of the conversation. "What? Who are you? I'm Jennifer Murphy, Sarah's mom."

He shook her hand. "Charlie Beckett."

Sarah took Charlie's money, a buoyant feeling in her chest. She felt like laughing, like joining in the car wash, throwing a bucket of bubbles over Franco, and drinking champagne. Maybe even flying to Costa Rica. "Potato salad, or chips?" She got out the paper plates and slid a savory cheeseburger on the toasted bun onto it.

"Chips." He continued talking to her mother. "Beckett Marketing. My dogs loved the treats."

"And you can get our Sarah's treats into stores?" her mom asked, handing Charlie a napkin wrapped around a fork and knife.

"This is surreal," Sarah said, daring to check out Franco from the corner of her eye.

He reached out and held her arm, caressing her skin with his thumb. "I told you. We make a good team."

"Are you sure you didn't pay him?" She had to know. It would be wrong, somehow, if he'd pulled extra strings.

"I can't afford him. If he likes your stuff, he takes a cut. He seems to know what the next trend will be and is right there on the first wave."

It was starting to sink in. "And he likes Happy Treats?"

"Loves them." Franco pointed to the people in line waiting for food now that the smell of searing meat had reached beyond the grill. "Let's do this."

"What about Charlie?" She glanced back at her mom and Leland who had Charlie seated at a picnic table.

"He will wait. He knows a good thing when he tastes it."

Sarah tossed her head back and laughed, letting the sheer joy of good fortune run through her body.

"It might not happen fast enough, though, to get the money for your roof." Franco studied her through the steam.

She looked at the line of people ready to buy burgers. Every little bit helped against the boxes of treats she had to sell. "It's okay, Franco. I have a plan. And it's coming together just fine."

She and Franco cooked burgers and hot dogs. Some people came back for more after tasting the seasoning on the meat. "What did you put in there?"

"Just a little something," he said, eyes twinkling.

Sarah pointed to the full cash box, which Leland had thankfully taken over. "I can't wait to see what we've got at the end of the day."

Franco asked, "What time is it, anyway?"

"Three o'clock. Are you ready to retire your apron?"

"We still have people to feed." He looked at her. "We work well together, don't we?"

She nodded.

"It's nice to be part of a team? To have a partner?"

"Yes!" He'd been stressing this partner thing all day. What did he want?

"Daddy! Sarah!" Bella barreled toward them with a fistful of balloons and cat eyes on each cheek. Martin followed behind, not looking quite as spry as he'd started the morning out.

Sarah chuckled and handed him a lemonade. "Thank

you for being in charge of the entertainment."

"Thank you, Martin," Franco said.

Her one and only employee raised his hand. "She is the cutest thing, Franco. But there is a reason I was never compelled to be a mother." He drank the lemonade. "I don't have the energy. I think I'll stick with my fur-babies and call it a day."

Franco laughed. "I like your face painting, Bella."

"Daddy, do you want some? The clown was really funny and told jokes. Want to hear?"

He nodded, giving Bella his full attention.

Bella looked at Martin, brow furrowed in concentration.

He whispered in Bella's ear and she stepped back, taking a deep breath as if ready to recite something.

"Why can't an egg tell a joke?"

Sarah and Franco looked at one another, and then shook their heads.

"Why?" Franco asked.

"Because it might crack up!" Bella bent over at the waist, laughing hard. "'Cause you crack an egg, get it, Daddy?"

"That's a good one, princess."

Martin and Sarah clapped. Leland came over, her mom and Charlie with him. "Sarah, why don't you and Franco take a break and talk with this marketing genius here. I can man the barbecue."

"I'll help," her mom said.

"Thanks. Let's go into the office," Sarah suggested. "Where we can talk in the air conditioning."

Charlie wiped his forehead on his sleeve. "Sounds great to me," he said. "This South Florida heat is killer on us red-heads."

Franco didn't move from his spot by the grill. "Are you sure, Sarah? I can wait out here if you'd like to handle this by yourself."

Sarah reached out for Franco's hand and pulled him beside her. "I would appreciate it if you'd come, too. I don't know what questions to ask a genius, and since you know him, you might steer me in the right direction."

His gaze warmed, making Sarah feel as if anything really was possible for them.

They went inside, where Benny and Pippa greeted them by the door. She'd kept Nashville at her apartment so the cat wouldn't get lost or frightened by the influx of people coming in and out.

Benny and Pippa had been trained to stay inside and wouldn't leave without her or being led by their leashes.

"These two are cute," Charlie said. "Could they be the faces of Happy Treats?"

"Sure," Sarah said. "Although Benny, the Chihuahua, is a little camera shy."

"The black one? She's got a beautiful face."

"Pippa. Bred for beauty, lacking in just about everything else." Sarah picked up the toy Pomeranian and tucked her under her arm. Charlie gave her a scratch behind the ears and she watched him fall in love.

"Is she for adoption?"

"She's mine." Sarah led the way to the kitchen. "This is where we made our first batch of treats. Franco helped me with the flavor combination."

Franco held out his hands. "This is all you, Sarah."

"It is us." She got out a pitcher of carrot juice and offered it around. "Charlie, what would be the next step, if we signed on with your company?"

"Well…"He noticed the rocket drawn on the poster board. "What's this?"

"I'm selling these treats, a box at a time, to get my new roof. I see that Martin has been keeping up on sales." She eyed the print on the side. The rocket was three quarters filled in. "Wow. I'm really close."

"I knew you could do it," Franco said. His deep voice was thick with emotion and Sarah turned toward him. "I am very proud of you."

Charlie sat down, smacking his palms against the table. "Are you two an item?"

Put on the spot and wanting to protect Franco, Sarah said, "No."

Staking his claim, Franco said, "Yes."

Charlie laughed. "This ought to be interesting."

Franco wished he could have some privacy with Sarah, to

convince her things would be all right. But no. He had to make his plea in front of Charlie. He'd given the marketing guru enough fodder for the gossip mill for another ten years.

In uncharacteristic Charlie-style, the man let him off the hook and stuck to business. "I have an artist on staff, a photographer. I see these treats have appeal to the people. You've done all of these sales in a week?"

"Yes," Sarah said. "Mostly. Desperation creates ingenuity."

"We don't want PetGiant getting your warehouse space," Charlie said. "You're going to need it for the animal shelter. I talked to the people supporting your event, and they like you Sarah. You have a place in the community."

Franco nodded. "It would be great to keep things local, and give back. Maybe Sarah can widen her jurisdiction?"

Sarah's face glowed with happiness. "I feel like this is a dream come true." She looked at Franco. "You made this happen, by believing in me. Thank you, Franco."

He was happy just to see her happy.

The chime above the door went off and the dogs barked, racing around the small kitchen table just in case Sarah hadn't heard the bell, they were going to let her know that someone was inside.

Franco leaned back to see who had come in, not recognizing the couple who had a giant Saint Bernard on a leash. A tall, thin woman stood with them, off to the side. Sarah grinned and got up, walking toward them with open arms.

"Karma! Joe. Princey!"

Benny and Pippa darted around the giant dog's paws, looking like chew toys in comparison. The big dog sprawled on the floor to get a better look and Pippa went nose to nose while Benny stayed at Sarah's feet.

"That could be a selling ad, right there," Charlie said. "I wish I had my camera."

"Karma, Joe, this is Charlie. My marketing genius," Sarah said with a laugh. She pulled Franco close, linking her arm through his. "And this is my partner, Franco de Silva."

"Partner?" Karma asked. She was a stylish blonde with an athletic figure and a great smile. "I remember when you told me you didn't have time for men."

Sarah flushed but waved the comment away. "It's complicated," she said.

"Changes by the minute," Charlie observed.

Joe had short dark hair, tattoos and a quick smile. "Nice to meet you both," he said. "This is our friend," he pulled the tall woman with caramel skin and high cheekbones forward, "Jolie Gordon. She runs a party charter."

"Nice to meet you," Jolie said. "I'd like to donate a charter to your fundraiser."

"Wow! Thank you," Sarah said. "I can tell we're

going to be great friends." The two women laughed, but Franco bet they probably would be. Jolie had an easy way about her that reminded him of Sarah, when Sarah was on the water.

Joe cleared his throat. "We wanted to say hi to Sarah, and order a dozen boxes of those treats. They ran out already." He jerked his thumb over his shoulder to indicate the table outside in the parking lot.

"You're kidding." Sarah nudged Franco. "I've got some in the warehouse. I think. I never thought I might run out."

He slid his arm around her shoulders, so proud of her. "The roof is a done deal."

"Celia told us how you were down to the wire," Karma said. "We wanted to show our support."

"My own fault. I kept wanting to do it all myself." She glanced up at Franco. "Instead of asking for a little help."

Franco slipped his arm around her waist.

Martin rushed in with Courtney. "Sarah, do we have any more treats? People are driving up from all over Broward County to help support the shelter."

"In the back. Thank you so much. Courtney, I don't what you did to get the news reporters here, but that has to be why, don't you think?"

Courtney grinned. "Human interest stories. The public loves them! They came back to do a follow-up. Girl, if you don't have these all sold, I'll eat my hat." She had her hair pulled back under a pink baseball cap with a sequined pelican above the brim. "They should be coming in, any minute now."

Martin, who'd run to the back, came out with a crate full of treats. "Sarah, this is the last hundred. I've been keeping up with the orders on the website, tagging them so that we'd know where we are." He fluttered his lashes. "We did it!"

"Uh, twelve of those are ours," Karma said. Princey sat up, Pippa between his paws, safely out of the way.

Franco chuckled. "I was going to offer to buy what was left, but I don't think there will be any."

Charlie slid Martin a ten and took a jar from the box.

Sarah threw her arms around Franco. "Thank you for believing in me." She lifted her face for a kiss just as the news reporter came into the office, camera flashing. Her mom, Bella and Leland were there too.

"Daddy and Sarah, sitting in a tree," Bella sang as her mom clapped and hooted.

Embarrassed, Sarah bowed her head into Franco's chest. "I guess we're an item," she said.

Franco tightened his hold, never wanting to let go.

His daughter gave him a happy grin, running over to grab his leg. He put his hand on her shoulder, and kissed Sarah's head.

"We are a team."

Chapter Twenty One

One month later

She had never seen the sky so blue. The air smelled salty sweet as pelicans flew above the clouds. Sarah sat next to Franco, shoulder to shoulder, on the beach blanket. They had a canopy for shade and a cooler of snacks Franco had prepared. Bella played with Madison, Bob's granddaughter from New York, in the surf.

"Now this is what I needed," Franco said, his leg stretched out next to hers.

"A morning away from the pet store?" Sarah asked, nudging his hairy big toe with her pedicured foot. She'd been taking some time for herself, remembering that she deserved some pampering too.

"No. You." He turned toward her, his dark eyes glinting. "I missed you. I don't like being away from you."

Sarah's heart welled with love. Learning about Franco, learning to care about another person as an equal partner, was teaching herself so much in the process. "Absence makes the heart grow fonder."

"That is bullshit, *querida*." He leaned over her as she sat back on the blanket, capturing her mouth in a kiss that left her wanting more. "Let's go to the Keys."

"Now?" Sarah laughed, loving his impetuosity. "I only have the day. The roof is done, Randall Wallace is off my case and there is no more talk of PetGiant. Not that anybody was supposed to be talking about it anyway. Small towns don't keep secrets very well."

"For our honeymoon."

Sarah's breath caught and she sat up so fast she pushed Franco backward. "Excuse me?"

He grinned, his dimple flashing. Reaching into the cooler, he handed her a miniature replica of the Happy Treat jar. "Open it."

Fingers trembling, Sarah slipped off the glass top. Inside the mini treats was a band of platinum. Simple. Exquisite. Classic.

She couldn't stop the tears spilling from her eyes as she took it out. "Franco, you shouldn't have."

"Will you marry me, Sarah? Be my partner in this crazy life? Since meeting you, loving you, I know what a relationship is supposed to be."

She looked out over the water, at Bella laughing with her friend. "Are you sure, Franco? What does Bella think?"

"She helped me pick out the ring. I wanted something with diamonds but she said you wouldn't wear it. She was right, I think."

"Pretty smart for a seven-year-old." Could she be a mother? A wife? They'd been inseparable, with the exception of sleepovers, making love in the day while Bella was at school. "I don't know how to be a mom." She clutched the glass jar.

"Saying yes means becoming a family. A mother. I can't imagine a more perfect woman to guide my daughter, to love her and show her how to be a strong woman, with heart. Like you."

Sarah sniffed as Franco slid the ring onto her finger. "I do love her. I love you." He tilted her chin up, staring into her eyes. "You've shown me that independent doesn't mean alone."

"Say yes," he asked, his deep voice rumbling over her. "You would make me the happiest man in the world."

"Yes."

His brown eyes brimmed with tears as he cupped the

back of her head and brought her close. "Thank you. I will never let you down."

Sarah curled her fingers over his bare shoulders, her hands warm against his skin. "Just don't stop kissing me." His kisses never failed to take her breath away.

With a low groan, he claimed her mouth, covering her lips with his. Velvet, firm. He made giving into temptation fun. With Franco at her side? Anything was possible.

MASQUERADE

by the Sea

Jolie Gordon grasped the edge of the captain's chair as her forty-foot pleasure cruiser rocked against a wave. Looking out from the cockpit, she searched the lightning-laced night sky for signs the storm was letting up. She braced for the next roll and patted her First Mate on the back. "Think they'll notice?" She looked behind her at the wedding party dancing below deck.

"Nope." Rajah Dubashi granted her a devilish grin. Midnight black eyes, coal-colored hair, her First Mate wore a hint of danger that was a hit with the ladies. "Just enough toasts to the bride and groom for the dip of the ocean to seem natural. They've all got their sea legs, or in this case, their champagne legs." He laughed, cracking himself up.

She leaned across Rajah and flipped on the high beams. Rain glinted in the shadows like an oil lamp against black velvet. Dark sea-green waves with white crests smashed over one another. They were in open water, with no other boats in sight. "We should keep close to the shoreline."

"What's the matter?" Rajah craned his neck to look at her. "The Masquerade's sturdy." He patted the beige chair. "She's seen her share of summer storms."

South Florida in June was hot, wet and tropical. Jolie rubbed her bare arms. "The skeleton I trust. It's the engine that's giving me hives. You know how damaging salt water can be to the filter. The seals are loose—" She balanced against the back of his chair, suddenly too hot as the list of things that needed fixing ran through her head.

"Before you have a melt-down, Captain, let me remind you that I checked it all out before we left." Rajah turned around and dimmed the lights. "Don't worry."

"It's my job." Jolie had inherited the thirty-year-old party charter from her grandfather, who would come back to haunt her if he knew she'd ripped out the paneling and installed hot pink faux fur and a disco ball.

She reached over Rajah's shoulder and tapped the screen on the digital satellite camera. "This storm cell came out of nowhere and doesn't look like it's dissipating anytime soon." Jolie checked the time on the brass clock next to the wheel. "Another hour until we dock. Hopefully our guests will have so much fun they'll never even know it rained."

"Tell Benedict to offer another round. This swell can pass as fast as it came in." Rajah drummed his hand against his leg. "They sound like they're having a good time."

High-pitched laughter bounded up the stairs during the breaks in music. Her bartender, Benedict Vonnigan, could make any mixed drink known to man while monitoring the party guests, adjusting music levels or sending the servers around with more drinks. "Let's keep them dancing," she said. *What will I do without Benedict?*

Rajah shimmied in his chair, tapping his feet to the beat.

Giving his moves a soft laugh, Jolie scanned the barely visible white caps of water from behind the enclosed plexi-glass. *If it would just stop raining.* "You all right?" She squeezed his upper arm.

"Go be the captain, Captain." Rajah flexed his grip on the wheel. "I'll try to keep the rolling to a minimum."

Jolie snagged the white hat from the hook by the threshold, adjusting the gold brim over her dark brown curls. "Thanks. If we dock too soon, they might feel cheated, and that is not what we're about." She left him in charge of navigation, and went down the stairs to the dance floor. "Happy, happy, happy."

She spied the bride, a cute blonde—Kendra—dancing with her bridesmaids while the darker-haired groom, Cody, finished his beer, setting the empty bottle on the bar and grinning as if he'd won the marital lottery.

Jolie excused herself through the crowd of dancers, bumping elbows and avoiding drinks, until she at last reached the oak bar and the magician behind it. Blond, dressed in black on black, and with a work visa that expired tomorrow.

"How's it going, Benedict?" She joined him, catching her three-inch heel on the tear in the rubber mat. Nobody else seemed to notice when the boat dipped.

"Good, Captain." Benedict poured white wine for two flushed and giggling women. He winked as they tipped him a five, making them giggle even more as they toddled off to join the other dancers. He bent his blond head toward her dark one and whispered, "Is it my imagination, or are we in the middle of some weather?"

Rajah and Benedict had been with her since she'd moved to this small town marina from Key West last year. The three of them made a great team but Benedict had to return home, to some city she couldn't pronounce, for the summer and she didn't have a replacement bartender. In denial, she'd been dragging her feet.

"You guessed it."

"Thought so." He handed the perspiring groom two chilled and uncapped beers before the man even asked.

"Thanks," Cody said, drinking deeply and swiping his brow with his forearm. Kendra tugged him close, stealing the other beer and resting her head against his shoulder.

Sweet. Jolie scanned the room, not seeing the groom's brother. Where was he?

The yacht pitched and Jolie quickly sprang into action as a few of the dancers stumbled. "How about another round of champagne? I can pour." She gestured to the two young women she'd hired to serve. One had auburn hair, the other firecracker red.

"Sure." Benedict reached behind him and took out six chilled bottles which he set down at her end of the counter. "I've got trays of flutes all ready to go."

"You're amazing." Her eyes welled. What *would* she do without him? The three of them covered all the bases in running the party charter. Rajah and Benedict both cooked, Rajah had mechanic experience and Benedict made her life easier with his efficient ways, ordering the fish and the booze.

Benedict wiped his hands on a bar towel. "I will be back before the holidays pick up and season starts."

They'd had this same conversation a dozen times. *Fine.* "I'll call a temp place tomorrow." Decision made, she uncorked the champagne and poured fizzy liquid into the flutes. The waitresses took trays as Benedict blew the sea horn and lowered the music.

"A word, from Captain Jolie Gordon!" Benedict introduced Jolie with a flourish.

She raised a flute toward the beaming couple and the servers quickly handed out the rest of the glasses. "To the newlyweds! Cody and Kendra Hamilton. May you live in peace, harmony and passion!"

Cody—a fireman—average in height but broad of shoulder, grinned and kissed his new wife on the lips. "Passion, you hear that, honey?"

Kendra grabbed him for another kiss and the room exploded with catcalls.

Benedict started the music again and the dancing erupted as almost forty people bounced around like human pogo sticks. Hardly a chance they'd notice the waves now. Jolie took another sip of the dry champagne, then settled back against the counter looking for Cody's brother.

Heath Hamilton was the taller of the two men, but slighter of build. Muscular without being pumped. Cody seemed easy-going despite the chaos of the wedding party, while Heath had a restrained demeanor, as if fun was a four letter word. She recognized in his solemn expression a man struggling with some inner demons.

Her chosen profession as hostess on the seas required keeping her guests happy. The fact that she found Heath's reticence a challenge prodded her to go in search of him.

She exchanged her champagne for a tumbler of ginger ale with a slice of lime. “Keep them dancing, Benedict. Ring the bell in forty-five minutes?” She liked a fifteen minute warning before they docked.

“Aye, aye Captain.”

First she checked the galley one floor under, then the heads, none occupied by Heath, and, really curious now, Jolie made her way through the dancers to the small, partially enclosed upper deck.

The wind off the ocean was brisk and she wished she’d grabbed a pashmina to cover her bare arms as she stepped onto the deck. She wore a neutral sheath that hit her knee, pearl accessories and nude heels. Inheriting her Jamaican Granny’s preference for bright colors, Jolie played her personal style to fit the occasion aboard the charter.

A gust of wind made her hair fly around her face, and she about lost her hat. *So much for style.*

“Are you all right?”

Jolie whirled toward the masculine voice, pulse racing. “I thought I was alone!” She peered into the shadows at the deck chairs covered by a canopy. “Heath? I was looking for you.”

“Why?” The question held suspicious undertones.

It’s my job. But it wasn’t just that, she admitted to herself. Jolie moved through the chairs to where he was stretched out on a lounger, tie loose but still around his neck, beer in hand, brown hair tousled over his brow. “I wondered if you'd give a toast to the bride and groom?"

She sat on the edge of the lounge chair next to his, figuring he had to be over six feet. No slouch in the height department at 5'9", Jolie was usually spot-on with her calculations.

"I gave one already."

"When?" She sipped her ginger ale, crinkling her nose as a bubble tickled the roof of her mouth. He didn't say much and she imagined how short and sweet his toast would have been. *Cheers. Bravo. Cool.*

"Earlier." He paused. "At the chapel."

"Oh." Jolie could tell he didn't want company, but she didn't want to leave him alone. "Can I get you another beer?"

He reached down beneath his suit coat, revealing two more frosty bottles, still capped. "I'm good for a while."

She laughed. He didn't.

Awkward. "So, what are you doing hiding away from the fun up here?"

He shot her a look, his eyes narrowed and glistening like polished amber. White lines bracketed his mouth. "I'm not a party kind of guy."

No kidding. "You don't have to dance if you don't want to." There'd been a time in her own life where just seeing other people happy added to her misery. What was his deal? Maybe he didn't like his new sister-in-law?

"Can't dance."

"The guys who say that are usually the best dancers," she teased.

"I *can't* dance." He pointed to his left leg. "Skiing accident."

Jolie eyed his legs. One was straight out, the other knee brought up. His injuries were hidden behind black slacks. "Water skiing?"

"Snow skiing in Utah. Nine months ago. I just finished physical therapy."

Three whole sentences, she thought. He had the lean muscle of an athlete. "Better in time for next year's ski season?"

"I won't ski again." His jaw clenched.

Well, hell. That hit a hot button. "It must have been a bad accident."

"I was a ski instructor. Ruined my damn life. Now, if you don't mind, Captain Jolie, I'd like to go back to my painkiller and beer buzz. The choppy waves aren't making my night any smoother."

Of course he'd noticed the storm. He couldn't miss it out here on the upper deck. The rain had slowed but lightning zapped its way between the stars like a pinball machine. "You don't feel it so much inside," she suggested.

"I need the fresh air." He swallowed and Jolie followed the movement of his Adam's apple.

"Seasick?" On top of injured, poor guy. No wonder he wasn't the life of the party. "I have some Dramamine downstairs."

"My beer is doing the trick."

The yacht swayed and his grip on the bottle tightened. Jolie had been raised on boats, so the roll of water was comforting, even during a storm. She waited in silence for a few minutes, wondering if Heath was always so angry or if it was the accident. He couldn't be a ski instructor without skiing. Where did that leave him?

She'd broken her arm once, falling off a dock, but at thirteen she'd been more worried about how the cast looked than any discomfort. Her mind skipped over a deeper pain that she'd learned to live with. She knew about starting over and redefining herself—it wasn't easy. "I'm sorry."

"Not your fault." Heath settled against the lounge chair and closed his eyes.

The rain stopped completely and the wind died down as if taking a break from its rage. She stepped to the railing and leaned back to study Heath. She'd never been drawn like this to a man, pulled by the heart strings. *I don't even know him.* Music sounded from below deck, drowning the chug of the yacht's engine.

"When do you go back to…Utah?" She sipped from her glass. He seemed like the kind of guy to face the elements and win.

Heath's eyes opened, dark honey in the starlight as he held her gaze. His gruff voice made her insides tingle. "Tomorrow."

Good. She'd save herself from making a mistake by going downstairs and doing her job. No flirting with the customers. He was leaving and she didn't do one-night stands. "I'll return you to your solitude," she said with forced brightness. "How long have you been here in South Florida?"

"A week. Kendra is from here." He drank, shifting on the lounger. "They're going to buy a place."

Jolie heard the sorrow in his voice and lingered. "You might have to learn how to water ski after all."

He grimaced. "Doubtful. Doctors tell me to be glad I can walk. Assholes."

Doctors had told her to try again, as if what she'd lost had little import. "They can be," she agreed. "Maybe you should stay on a week or so. My cousin does aquatic physical therapy, which is a lot less stressful on your body. It might help your leg, if you're still in pain."

"I'm not staying. I belong in the mountains." He emptied his beer and switched it out for a full one. "Or I did." He stared down at the bottle. "Damn if I know where I'm supposed to be at the moment."

Jolie cradled her glass of ginger ale to her chest so that she didn't reach out and smooth Heath's hair back from his forehead. She'd been where he was sitting, at a crossroads. "What will you do when you get back home?"

He scooted back and sat up, stretching out both legs with a wince. "Find a new physical therapist, since my brother just married mine." His mouth twisted wryly.

Balancing with the roll of the yacht, Jolie finished her ginger ale and swirled the ice in the glass. "Woops. What will you do for work?" It seemed a shame for an outdoors guy like Heath to be stuck with an office job. But it might be best for his leg.

"Got something lined up. Doesn't start 'til October, though."

"What?" Computer stuff, maybe?

"Virtual skiing. Since I can't do the real thing." He shrugged, his tone bitter. "I've been on skis since I could walk. The smell of fresh snow, the bite of the wind against your face as you're flying down the slope, there's nothing like it."

"I've never snow skied, but you sound like you love it. I bet you were a great teacher." Heath's strong features and cocoa brown hair had probably garnered him his share of snow bunnies.

"Instructor. Yeah." He tugged at his loose tie, as if uncomfortable at her praise. "Tell me about the Masquerade, Captain Jolie. I don't hear an accent. You from the Caribbean?"

She guessed he didn't like the attention being on him, which made him practically chatty. Jolie lifted a strand of shoulder-length kinked hair. "Jamaica."

"Born there?" Heath drank, absently massaging his left leg.

"Yes, but then we moved to the Keys when I was three." Her family had traded one tropical port for another. "My grandfather built boats."

"This one?" He reached down to give the deck a pat.

"Yes." Memories of Gramps with his smiling brown eyes and warm calloused hands washed over her and she had to clear her throat. "The Masquerade was his pride and joy," she managed.

He nodded. Thumping bass and laughter from below deck complemented the flutter of wind against the canopy and the slap of waves on the hull. Her grandfather had preferred fishing charters and Styrofoam coolers full of bait to gourmet appetizers. Beer over champagne.

"He must be gone, then?" Heath asked.

Jolie was surprised when her eyes watered. She shifted from one foot to the other, then decided to just slip off her heels. Her bare feet connected to the deck, giving her instant peace. "Two years ago."

"Did he know what you were going to do to his boat?"

She glanced at Heath, stunned by the gentleness in his teasing smile. As if he understood her pain, too, and shared it. It transformed him from angsty and rugged to downright sexy.

Heavy, dark brown brows over compassionate eyes. Clean shaven hours ago when she'd first noticed him coming aboard with the other wedding guests, now there was stubble along his jaw. Her fingers ached to touch the rough skin. To know the texture of the dip of his throat.

She looked away, caught in her own fantasy. "You

must have been reading my mind." Jolie curled her toes against the damp deck, anchoring her emotions. Something about Heath reminded her of how far she'd come. "I was just thinking about how much he'd hate what I've done to her." Jolie shook her head and stared at the melting ice in her glass. But she had to make a living, too—and she wasn't in to sports fishing.

"Want me to get you another drink?" he asked, sliding his legs over to the side of the lounge chair.

"No! Stay there, Heath, you're a guest." And injured. "It's just ginger ale. Doesn't normally make me sad." She lifted the glass.

"I'm fine," he said, his brow raised in disbelief. "You run a party boat and you don't party?"

"I like to party," Jolie said, remembering huge fish bakes with all the trimmings. The sense of togetherness that came from laughing and having a good time with family and friends. "Love it. It's what made me switch the Masquerade from fish to fun. I just like to save the drinking for when I'm not Captain."

"That's smart." Heath tilted his head, his eyes turning a lighter shade of amber as the moon came out from behind a cloud. *Dry skies, thank God.* Heath asked, his lips curved upward, "Did you have to go to Captain school?"

"There are tests, yes." She touched the patch above the brim of her white hat, returning his smile. "The Coast Guard has regulations to become a commercial licensed yacht operator." Shrugging one shoulder she added, "But I've been running this boat since I was five. Gramps would stand me up on the old wooden captain seat and put my hands on the wheel. Told me I could go wherever I wanted, and don't let anybody tell me different."

"He seems like a great guy."

"I've been blessed with a wonderful family." They'd given her space when she needed it, and loved her as she found her way to the other side. "What about you?"

"Just me and Cody left. And now he's moving here."

A wave lifted the prow and Jolie braced herself, leaning back with her elbows. She hated the idea of Heath returning to an empty place with nothing to fill the time but sad memories. "Please tell me you aren't going to sit in a ski lodge somewhere and re-live your glory days," she said, mostly joking.

He scowled. "That's not the plan."

"Good."

"I bartended through college. Made a promise to myself that I'd never be that sad old dude with his own bar stool lost in a whiskey."

Jolie gripped her empty ginger ale glass, setting it at her bare feet. He'd bartended? She held onto her captain's hat and tipped back to stare up at the stars. *Are you kidding me?* She believed in things happening for a reason. Universal signs.

But how could he handle being at the bar for hours at a time? A stool might help. And the longest shift would be about four hours, tops. She had to replace the mat behind the bar anyway—she'd get a thicker one for better support.

No. Heath would be a liability. But...

"I hated it," he said. She slumped, then he added, "Loved it too." Heath rolled the bottle between his hands as if starting a fire. "I like finding out what makes people tick. There's a lot going on inside the inebriated mind that only comes out when the inhibitions are down. When the mask comes off."

She laughed softly, understanding what he meant. "Just mellow enough for true colors to show."

"Exactly." Heath sat back, crossing his legs at the ankles. He'd kept his shiny black shoes on. "I doubt we'd ever have had this conversation if I'd been completely sober."

"You don't look drunk," Jolie said. No slurred speech or drowsy eyes.

"I'm not. Can't afford to break my other leg." He winked and lifted his beer bottle.

Another joke? He intrigued her, plain and simple. She took a deep breath and pushed away from the railing, the soles of her feet absorbing the coolness of the polymer deck. "I can't believe I'm going to suggest this," she said. It was crazy, *crazy*, but it might suit each of them.

He cocked his head. "What?"

"It sounds like you need a job."

His warm amber eyes hardened. "You heard wrong.

I've got money."

She held up her hand, retreating to start again. "Not a job, then, but something new to shake you out of your winter-time mountain rut."

"I don't understand." Heath sat forward, his gaze curious and cautious.

"I need a bartender. Just until September. You'd have plenty of time to get back to Utah for your other job." Jolie nodded even as he looked at her like she was nuts. *Maybe I am.* "Benedict leaves tonight, after this cruise. Just for a couple months and he'll be back. You'd be doing me a huge favor." She gave him her most imploring smile.

"Forget it." He sat back, his expression closed.

"You don't even want to talk about it?" She patted his right shoe and walked toward the door leading down to the party. The music. The fun. She'd prefer to stay up here and talk with him. "The pay isn't great, but it's free room and board." Jolie sent him a conspiratorial look. "All the cake you can eat after the parties we book."

"No, thanks." He didn't budge. "People don't up and move without any notice."

Jolie had an ever-expanding list of things to fix, but this just might solve a few. She needed a bartender, Heath had some free time. If he could cook, it'd be perfect. "Think about it, Heath. What do you have to lose?"

Continue reading MASQUERADE by the Sea

Go to ReadByTheSea.com

A Note From the Author

Thank you for reading Puppy Love by the Sea.

I healed in Lauderdale by the Sea after my personal life was turned upside down. The ocean's tranquility gave peace during a tumultuous time. My hope is that these stories will offer a soothing seaside escape and a continued belief in happily ever after.

If you enjoyed this book, help others find it so they can enjoy it too.

- **Recommend it:** Please help other readers find this book by recommending it to friends, readers' groups, and discussion boards.
- **Review it:** Let other potential readers know what you liked about this book.

If you'd like to sign up for Traci Hall's newsletter to receive new release information, please visit TraciHall.com

About the Author

With an impressive bibliography in an array of genres, USA Today bestselling author Traci Hall has garnered a notable fan base. She pens stories guaranteed to touch the heart while transporting the reader to another time and place. Her belief in happily ever after shines through, whether it's a romantic glimpse into history or a love affair for today.

Find Traci online at:
TraciHall.com
Twitter.com/TraciHallAuthor
Facebook.com/BytheSeaSeries

Printed in Great Britain
by Amazon

87068645R00173